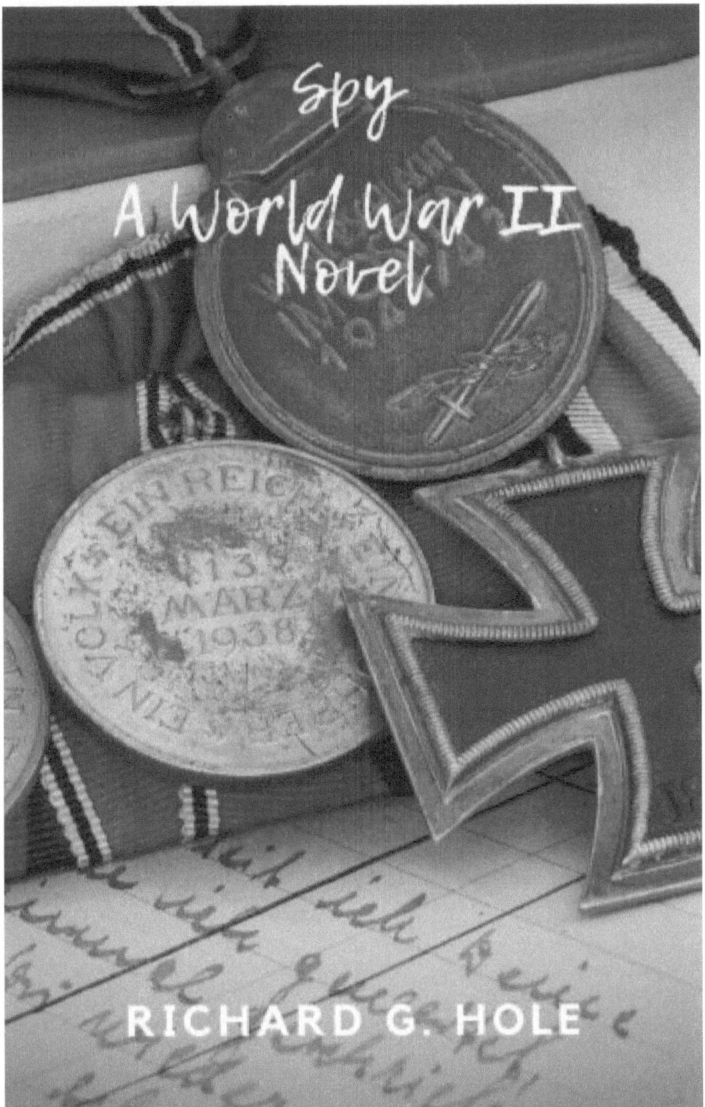

Spy
A World War II
Novel
RICHARD G. HOLE

Spy
A World War II Novel

Richard G. Hole

World War II

SUMMARY

In the early morning of September 1, the loudspeakers of the different units of the barracks began to howl.

They all raised their heads, startled.

The announcer announced that the German Führer was going to speak to his people.

And then they heard the news.

The German army, ignoring its ultimatum, had just crossed the Polish border.

Spy is a story belonging to the World War II collection, a series of war novels developed in World War II

SPY

The bar was one of many as can be found in Soho. A nondescript place, frequented by dubious people and subject to frequent searches by the police. At that time, five thirty on a cloudy and still a bit cold spring afternoon, it was almost empty. It was not until a little later, after tea, that the regulars would begin to arrive.

The man entered the bar, leaned over the counter, and ordered whiskey. The innkeeper served it casually, and the man drank it in small sips, looking around. Only three people, besides him, were in the place, and none seemed the one he was looking for.

Around six o'clock the customers began to arrive. They ordered their drinks and consumed them with thirsty speed. It was around ten past six when someone approached the man and stood next to him.

"Beer" he asked. Then he turned to the other.

"Good night. You don't know me, but I do.

"Are you the one who called me on the phone?

"Yes.

He spoke in a low voice. He was of medium height, with a large head and a strong neck. Close-cropped dark blond hair grew hispid over his head. His eyes were blue and staring.

"What do you want? Asked the one who arrived first.

He was considerably younger than the newcomer. About twenty-eight years old. Correct features, blond hair and tall stature. He was slim, but strong.

"Not here. We will go elsewhere to talk. If you don't mind, "he added politely.

"No, of course, but I can't waste much time.

"I assure you that you will not lose it. Drink that and let's go.

The younger one shrugged slightly and obeyed. A moment later they were out on the street.

Across the street from them was a movie theater. The shorter one turned to his partner.

"That cinema is almost always empty in its back rows. We can talk quietly.

"Is it necessary so much luxury of precautions?

"It is. I don't want someone to hear what I have to say to him.

They took out the localities and entered the cinema. Indeed, the seats in the back were empty. On the screen, followed with little interest by the viewers, unfolded the misadventures of the invisible man.

"Well, what do you want?

The second man lit a cigarette, after offering another to his partner.

His name is Helmuth Frick.

"Did you bring me here to tell me that?

"Not. But I want you to know that I know your personality. You are an engineer and have been with the Magnus Corporation for two years.

"Good," Helmuth said.

And finally, you are German.

"Yes. And now tell me who you are. Otherwise, I will leave the cinema. You are well informed about me, but that is not enough to hold my attention for longer than two more minutes.

"My name is Loewe, Karl Loewe.

"I'm sorry, that name doesn't tell me anything, except that ...

Except I'm also German. I can't tell you where I work, at least for now. But I and... other people want to ask you to do something.

"What?

"You will find out tomorrow, if you go to the Embassy. You have to renew your passport. That will be a good excuse to show up there. Once your document has been renewed, ask for me. They will instantly bring you into my presence. We wish it were you without fail, Herr Frick. I hope it will.

"Can't you tell me anything about...?

"No, Herr Frick. I am sorry. But see me tomorrow at the Embassy and we can have an interesting talk. It will?

"Listen, Herr Loewe, what you are asking of me is...

"It's official, we might say, Herr Frick. It is not an order, of course, but we would be very sorry if you did not attend that interview.

Loewe got to her feet.

"And now" he added in a low voice and without inflection, "I must withdraw. Tomorrow at eleven o'clock, don't forget, Herr Frick. Stay even for a while at the cinema, don't immediately come out after me.

He left. For a further quarter of an hour, Helmuth followed the invisible man on the screen, until death surprised him in the laboratory and began to embody his fleshly shell. Then Frick came out.

In Piccadilly he had a bite to eat at one of the Lyon restaurants, but could hardly have said what. Kronen's words, two months ago, were still ringing in his ears, rekindled by this afternoon's interview.

"What I don't understand," Wilhelm Kronen, who worked as a chemist at a major English company, had told him, "is how they haven't tried to contact you yet. Things are very dark, Helmuth, and they are using all the means at their disposal ".

Well, they had already contacted him.

And by certainly quite twisted means.

He finished eating. It was almost time for the appointment with Iolande. He had just enough time to wait for her at the subway exit. Walking slowly, he headed toward Leicester Square.

The next morning, Saturday, he left the family pension he was occupying on Tavistock Street, near the Strand, and headed for the Embassy. The mist of the previous day had lifted, and a clear sun was shining on the Thames, lending its dirty waters a charm they ordinarily lacked.

The German Embassy was in Carlton House Terrace, near Mali. It was an old building, very spacious, within which an almost perfect order reigned. He went to the passport department and the clerk renewed hers, with a smile. They already knew each other before. Then, with an air that he tried to be as nonchalant as possible, he asked for Herr Karl Loewe.

He was guided to a small office, located in one of the corners of the building. Loewe himself was waiting for him, sitting behind the table. He stood up and said, raising his arm:

"Heil, Hitler!

Then, in a more normal voice:

Please sit down, Herr Frick. I thank you very much for your visit.

"Actually," said Helmuth, "a simple official note would have been enough to remind me that I had to renew my passport to ...

Loewe interrupted him without violence, but with authority.

"No, no, Herr Frick; I'm sorry, but it's better this way.

Right now, Helmuth thought. "As usual. If things can be done in a twisted way, why do things normally? "

But he was silent, waiting for the other to speak.

"Herr Frick, we are aware of your work at the Magnus Corporation. We know... we really know everything that concerns you. You won't waste a lot of time, nor will I lose you. Having established that premise, I will go on to tell you what we expect ... what Germany expects of you.

Helmuth bowed his head.

"You will receive within a month the annual leave to which you are entitled under British labor laws, will you not?

"Indeed.

"Have you already thought about how you will use that free time?

"I had planned to take a short trip to Germany and spend the rest touring the country of Wales.

Loewe nodded.

"Excellent. But we ... that is, our country, expect you to provide certain services.

He's out now, Helmuth thought uneasily.

"And good?

"We would be extremely pleased if you would give up that trip to Germany and the walk through Wales. You will not lose your vacation, of course. The places you could go have as many attractions and beauties as Wales. We regret to ask you to deprive yourself of a short and well-deserved trip to the Homeland, but I can assure you that it would appreciate much more if you followed our instructions.

"What should I do?

Loewe handed him a piece of paper on which he had written several names. Helmuth glanced at him. They were English populations, located in the north and center of the country. He looked up questioningly.

"Do you want to ask something, Herr Frick? Any clarification?

"Yes. Know what exactly is expected of me.

For a moment, Loewe seemed to hesitate.

"You are a good German, Herr Frick. You have done part of your studies in this country, but you are a good German, right?

"I think so.

"Well, we don't have any reason to doubt it either. That is why we have not hesitated to take this step, which I dare say may have great significance for our country.

He paused, lighting a cigarette. Helmuth smoked, too, slowly.

"In all those places, Herr Frick, there are things that may interest Germany. They are things of a very diverse nature, but equally interesting from the point of view … let's say political.

Helmuth looked him squarely in the eye.

"You have just done me the honor of considering me a good German, Herr Loewe. I think you can speak frankly. From a military point of view, perhaps?

Yes, Herr Frick. From a military point of view, too.

But I don't have access to British secrets.

"Needless. That is what specialized people do. Your mission will consist of photographing, with your tourist machine, bridges under construction or already built, railway junctions, places that could serve as a concentration of troops, both line and mechanized, airfields that can be used militarily, and so on. With regard to bridges, in his capacity as an engineer he can make some calculations that allow us to know their capacity to resist traffic, their density of construction, materials and strength of the same, etc. You see that we are not asking for the impossible, but only for a small personal effort in the undesirable case that world events lead to armed conflict.

"I understand" said Helmuth. Good, Herr Loewe. Suppose... suppose the mission was not to my liking. Suppose I was not inclined to undertake it.

"That probability has not even crossed our minds, Herr Frick, I must admit.

"But, in case it were so ...

"In that case, you would be very free to make a decision according to your wishes.

She was looking at him with eyes that had lost all friendly expression, and Helmuth realized it.

"But... Herr Frick, my superiors would not welcome your intention to continue in Great Britain. As a reserve officer of the Reserve, you would be called upon to join a unit. But we must not face unpleasant possibilities. I am sure, given your background, that you will not refuse to collaborate in the defense of our homeland. And so I have made it known, anticipating this interview, to my superiors.

There was no way out. Or go back to Germany to be incorporated into any of the army units or do what they asked him to do. The thing was perfectly clear.

Apart from the fact that how would Fraülein Zermatt take such an unpatriotic attitude?

Why are you mixing Fraülein Zermatt into this? Helmuth asked dryly.

"Just as a possibility. The possibility that Fraülein Iolande Zermatt was inclined to regard you as a man somewhat unworthy of having set her beautiful eyes on him.

"Is it a threat, Herr Loewe?

"Nerd! In any way. It is just that, a possibility. Fraülein Zermatt has always shown herself to be an excellent patriot.

"I want to tell you one thing," Helmuth said slowly. There is nothing that I would not do for my country, if it asked me to. But I don't want to be coerced at all. Whatever I do for him, I will do it of my free will and not under threat of any kind. Is this clear?

"Completely. And believe that I thank you ... that we appreciate your sincerity. A man who makes such a clarification, we believe that he is safer than another who would have committed without hesitation.

"That is the case, as far as me is concerned.

"So Herr Frick, can we close the deal?

Helmuth hesitated slightly. Very slightly, but Loewe noticed.

"Is there something we should know, Herr Frick?

"Nothing, other than that I would not like to go to war with this country. Here I have found work ...

"That he had not lacked in Germany, I hasten to clarify.

"Okay, so be it. Let me finish. I have found work and I have friends. Not many, but some, and they seem sincere. I must also add that, in the event of a conflict, I would not hesitate for a single second, of course. My homeland is Germany and I would fight for it. With this I just want to explain that I would not like to have to go to the last extreme, but that, if necessary, I would. Have I explained myself well, Herr Loewe?

"With excellent clarity. Those objections, that sense of friendship, honor him and make me feel more satisfied than ever to be able to count on the collaboration of a man who is not a mercenary, but a conscious patriot and imbued with his sacred duties.

He extended his hand across the table. Helmuth found it slightly soft and not at all energetic, but he shook it.

He rose to his feet, imitated by Loewe.

"Another thing, Herr Frick. Naturally, all of this will bring you some extra expenses, which the German government will gladly pay for. A checking account will be made available to you at the Mediterranean Bank, from which you can use without unnecessary waste "Germany is not rich, you know", but not without miserliness. I can assure you that, trusting you, that account will not be subject to supervision. Germany is not rich, I repeat, but it knows how to take care of those of its children who work for it.

As Helmuth was about to speak, he raised his hand admonitory in the air.

"No, Herr Frick. This is not a payment. It is simply not depriving you of your savings. You can use that account as you like. Unscrupulous, who, even when they honor you, are out of place. We do not pay an employee, we ensure the comfort of a collaborator.

And when they went out:

"In fifteen days from today, that is, June 2, come see me. A certain person will give you complete instructions. Goodbye, Herr Frick, Heil Hitler!

His outstretched hand almost got between Helmuth's eyes. He saluted a little less theatrically and left the office.

"But, dear" objected Iolande, "I thought we would go to Germany. I was really looking forward to going there, together with you, and for you to meet my parents.

"I am sorry.

They were in Hyde Park, sitting on a bench, warming themselves in the warm May sun. A little further on, perched on a packing crate, a smug-faced man spoke tirelessly to a small group of idlers. Snippets of his sentences came from time to time, carried by the wind, to the ears of both young Germans.

"... And I assure you, dear brothers, that the final hour is drawing near. That Christ will come down from the clouds, like a thief in the night, and woe to those who were not prepared to receive him! ...

"Yes, you are sorry, but you don't give me any explanation.

Iolande's hair was so blond that it almost looked white in the sun. His complexion pale from the recent winter; her red mouth, very little painted, and her blue dress, were very nice to see. Helmuth was looking at her with narrowed eyes. She was beautiful and he loved her. He wanted to marry her and live in some small town, in Germany or in England, a simple life, without complications, and, above all, without those dark clouds that loomed on the horizon.

"... Be prepared, brothers, I beg you earnestly! Do not sleep! Be vigilant! Always vigilant to await His arrival...!

"Sorry, Iolande.

"But at least" she replied with a new note in her voice "could you give me an explanation.

Helmuth hesitated for a moment.

"Iolande, do you think there will be war?

"I don't want it and I don't know if there will be or not. I am not a politician, but a girl who works for a living. But what does that have to do with ...?

"One moment. You don't want there to be a war, but if there was... what would you do?

"Helmuth, I find you very dark today. I want you to tell me exactly what you are thinking.

"In the war. In the possibility that there is.

Answer, Iole. Believe it or not, it is related to what we are talking about.

"If there were," she replied slowly, fiddling with a ribbon from her dress, "I would try to go to Germany, if I had time, and do what they ordered."

I lift my gaze to him.

And now, explain yourself. If you want.

"You see, Iole. I know you don't hate the English. You live here and work with them, just like me. We would not like either of us to have to fight, either indirectly, against this nation. Unfortunately, it is not in our power to prevent war from breaking out. We are a couple of units in the midst of forces over which we have not the least power.

"Why don't you get to the point? I am not in the mood to endure philosophical-political lectures at this time.

His voice was full of disappointment. They had planned many times that trip to Germany, in which they would announce to Iolande's parents, in Kiel, their engagement. Helmuth had no family.

"To the point I'm going. My dear, I do not know if I am wrong or wrong to tell you, but the fact is that I have been asked in an official way to spend my holidays in this country.

"But... for what purpose? Why do they get into ...? Asked Iolande, her eyes widening. His eyebrows, so pale they were barely visible from the rest of his face, were arched.

Helmuth threw discretion to the wind. After all, he hadn't been forbidden to speak to his fiancée.

He explained it to her. When he finished, she said only:

"Understand.

Then, after a moment, so long that he almost had time to smoke a whole cigarette, he added:

"The point is that I didn't want to go to Germany alone. Do you see any difficulty in me making that trip with you?

Helmuth hesitated for a moment.

"I don't see any, like that from first intention, but would they like it?

"I don't know, and the point is that I don't care either. Helmuth, since we have screwed up our trip to Germany, let's do that together. Do not say no to me. If you have not been prohibited, you can do it. I'll consider it a personal offense if you don't.

Helmuth smiled.

"Well. We will do one thing. When I go to see them I will ask you in secret. I don't think it matters either.

"We could even pass for husband and wife. This would arouse less suspicion, should we arouse any.

The idea was becoming more and more attractive to Helmuth.

"Okay, as long as they don't put a heavy load on it.

"They have forced you to do it under duress, haven't they? Well, they will have to put up with it.

The speaker had gotten out of his drawer and carried it; he walked away amid the indifference of his listeners. The afternoon was waning. It smelled of laurel and cinnamon.

"Okay," Helmuth said. And now we go where I can kiss you. If we were in Paris, I would do it right here Unfortunately ...

They walked away, arm in arm, followed by the unapologetic glances of spinsters pulling their dogs.

On June 2, Helmuth was greeted by Herr Loewe and a man in plain clothes, but of unmistakably military bearing. He was dry, with such abrupt manners, that he nearly made Helmuth lose patience several times. He held back with an effort. His interlocutor was pointing out in the various cities the places that he should visit and the details of which he had to take note. He was very thorough in his explanations and Helmuth realized that he was a man very used to such things. He was a military man, but also a technician, perhaps an engineer. At last he was alone with Loewe.

"I don't need to tell you that you shouldn't take a written note of any kind, not even in numbers. Because you are German (you must not hide your nationality in any way), you can be registered if you instill any suspicion. Everything must be kept in your head. How much memory do you have?

"Good," Helmuth replied dryly.

"Excellent, according to his teachers and former classmates. Don't be modest, my dear Herr Frick. All of this will be child's play for you.

Helmuth attacked head-on.

"Fraülein Zermatt wants to accompany me on this journey.

Loewe's eyes narrowed slightly.

"Have you updated him on our conversation?

"Of course not," Helmuth lied. " But we had a trip to Germany planned and this has come to spoil it, as you know. She doesn't want to be separated from me.

"I find it very reasonable. Take it, dear friend. A woman is an excellent excuse to take pictures. They are so beautiful in their charming postures when behind there is a bridge, a dam, a railway station...! Photographing them in front of a battleship is a pleasure to behold! You must definitely wear it.

"Thank you," Helmuth muttered in bewilderment. This little man seemed to be guessing her ideas.

"I will," he replied.

"Fraülein Zermatt is therefore also included in our expense account. We hope, dear friend, that you do not take advantage of it to completely renew your wardrobe, "he added with thick laughter.

And giving him a friendly pat on the back, she walked him to the door. There the Heil Hitler roared! and Helmuth left the embassy.

Helmuth's vacation began on the twentieth. He had been warned that he should no longer appear at the embassy, since everything had already been discussed. He didn't, then. On the 20th they took the train to Manchester and there they began their route throughout the north of England, the south of Scotland and then back, slowly, along the east coast. Manchester, Leeds, Newcastle, Scarborugh ...

It was a very happy few days. Helmuth had decided from the beginning to pose as newlyweds. This made the fellow trainers, the residents in the hotels, leave them relatively quiet. Nor did they shy away from the company. They couldn't do it, lest they arouse certain suspicions. As the world situation was, with changes of notes between Germany and France and England, virulent speeches by "boebbels", threats to Poland, a German couple was not, even for the quiet English, as unnoticed as a year would have been. before.

They were, therefore, very courteous, without exaggerating the note; they took long walks on the outskirts of the cities, they made excursions to the Pennines, always with their cameras on their shoulders. But they did not develop the photographs anywhere, instead they kept the reels until they could deliver them in London.

In the evenings, Helmuth, on a piece of paper that he later destroyed, took notes of everything he had seen and studied it carefully. The length of the bridges on the main highways, the weight they could bear, their foundations, the state of conservation of the roads, the approximate dimensions of the airfields, to which they went as simple and admired tourists to watch the planes leave. ...

All this he studied with a mind trained by his profession. Then he burned the papers and only kept a harmless travel diary, very typical of a newlywed, in which he wrote down the places they had passed, without any more details than some sentimental details that Iolande was in charge of adding. Those names would be enough to later remember where the photographs belonged.

Finally, on July 15, they returned to London. Helmuth was due to return to work two days later, on the 17th. On the 16th, he went to the Embassy and met with Loewe. He picked up the spools of photographs and then passed them on to the military man, whose name Helmuth did not know.

The photographs were developed in no time and then Helmuth settled in front of a large table, with the military man on the other side, and began the explanation.

Slowly, trying not to keep anything in his memory, he made what could be called the technical history of the trip. A device was recording his statements, while the military verified data and examined the photographs. All of this kept them busy all day and part of the night. Finally, at half past ten, they finished.

The military man stood up, lighting a cigarette.

"In principle, very good. Good amateur work, Herr Frick.

"I'm sorry" Helmuth replied annoyed. I've done my best. I am certainly not a professional.

"I did not mean to offend him. The work you have done is good enough that I do not hesitate to congratulate you.

"Thanks.

The soldier rose to his feet and Helmuth followed suit.

"While you were out of London some things have happened... Some things not completely unforeseen. Herr Frick, I'm afraid you'll have to go home.

"When? Helmuth asked with a frown.

"Soon. We will surely receive the order one of these days. You are a reservist for military engineers, aren't you?

"Yes sir.

"With the rank of second lieutenant.

"That's how it is.

"They are calling the reservists for summer maneuvers. I tell you even though it is a secret, because it will soon cease to be, and I see no reason to keep it from you.

A kind of cold snake ran down Helmuth's back. There it was already, then.

"But I have already passed the five years of annual internships. Does this ... does this mean war?

"Let's hope not" replied the other with an expression that denoted the opposite. An icy expression had appeared in his pupils. " But Germany can no longer endure interference with our destiny. No, Herr Frick, and you know that very well.

Helmuth thought that once Czechoslovakia and Austria had been annexed, Hitler said that the German claims were over. That, at least, emerged from his speeches. But it did not seem to be the most opportune occasion to say it. He just looked at the other, waiting.

"They will soon send you the summons. Anyway, you've already had a great vacation. Not everyone can say the same there, in the homeland.

She walked him to the door.

"Goodbye, Second Lieutenant Frick.

Helmuth sensed the Herr's suppression, but said nothing. The thing, then, was serious.

People on the street did not seem to pay any attention to the new events. They all appeared calm, but Helmuth was not. For an instant, a certain feeling of pride washed over him. Those English ... they were on the edge of a volcano and, nevertheless, they continued walking through the streets with impassive faces, drinking their tea, reading their Times ...

Instead, Germany was preparing. The immense factories of Essen spewed out hundreds, thousands of cannons daily; The Skoda, in Czechoslovakia, fed the green hordes with machine guns, millions of rifles, thousands of planes... The most formidable industrial power in the world was looming over the borders.

Then pride gave way to fear. Not physical fear for the approach of war, but the healthy fear of losing a position that he liked and in which he earned money, compassion for the number of women who would be left without husbands, boyfriends, brothers, and father; the millions of boys, the flower and the promise of so many countries that would die ...

When he met Iolande, who was waiting for him in the hall of the small family hotel, he took her by the arm and led her out into the street. The taverns, pubs, and bars had already closed, but that didn't matter, because it was a gorgeous summer night.

When he finished explaining it to her, she was silent for a moment.

"When do you think they will call you?

"I do not know. They haven't told me.

"I guess... I guess I'll have to go too.

"Yes, but they won't call you. You are not a reservist.

She didn't smile.

"The point is that now I can't quit my job.

Iolande was employed in an insurance office, a very reputable Swiss house in London. She was the secretary to one of the directors and made a lot of money. He doubted they would give him that much in Germany.

"Well, I don't think there is much of a hurry for you to leave the country. With being prepared in case things go wrong at some point, I think there will be enough.

She was silent for another moment. He seemed to go to say something, but then fell silent. He didn't speak for almost five minutes.

"Well, I suppose in Germany secretaries will also be needed. The point is, Helmuth, I don't want to leave you.

They walked arm in arm down the street, very close together.

"Don't think I don't like the idea either, but what can we do? Wait. Don't quit your job yet. It can be a false alarm, like when it happened in Munich a year ago.

"What if it is not? I'd like to go with you in case they call you, Helmuth.

"Wait honey. They haven't called me yet. Some patience:

She sighed.

"Well. We will wait, but I'm going to think about it. Helmuth, why don't we get married? We know that we love each other and that together we are happy. Why wait any longer?

"To fatten our savings.

"They will be of little use to us if war breaks out.

"You will see how in the end everything is a false alarm. He accompanied her home and then returned to the hotel.

Reserve 2nd Lieutenant Helmuth Frick was called on July 30. The general mobilization had not yet been decreed and, therefore, it was not by an order by which he was called, but an indication that he had to report to Germany, in Darmstadt, to do his annual military exercises, of which he was exempt for five years. But now he knew that it was a plain and simple mobilization.

"When do you have to join? Asked Iolande, her eyes dry, but the hand with which she was holding the cigarette trembling.

"I have to be in Darmstadt on August 3.

Just enough time to pack and take the boat.

He clapped his hands on the table. They were in a bar in Whitechapel, drinking beer and eating salty donuts.

"This will make me lose my job, Iole. Naturally, when they gave it to me they had no idea that it could be called from Germany at any time. I don't think they will be amused.

He did not do it. The Magnus chief of staff shook his head sullenly. Of course, Helmuth hadn't told him why he had to go to Germany when he had just returned from the holidays, but he smelled it.

"What are you guys up to? He asked sternly. I am not referring to you, but to Germans in general. Anyone would say they'd like to get into another ruckus like the one in 1914.

"I don't know, sir. My motives are familiar, as I have already told you.

"Well, I can't hold it, naturally; but neither can I assure you that your position will be vacant in a month or two. The Magnus is a serious company. Fulfills your requests and is considerate of your employees, but requires reciprocal behavior from them.

"I am sorry.

"Well; if there is no other remedy, leave, but your position will most likely be taken when you decide to return.

He got paid, said goodbye to the chief engineer, who asked him if they earned salaries as important as in England, and added that those damn Nazis were all crazy, starting with the house painter who shouted at them from the radio . Finally, he took the train.

"I wish I had gone with you," Iolande told him when she said goodbye to him at Victoria station.

There was a new expression in his eyes that Helmuth could not analyze at that moment.

"If things get bad, pack the mat and come back" he said, hugging her. But in the meantime, I think you'll be better off here.

"I don't know," she replied, kissing him so hard that it hurt. " I do not know. But be careful, Helmuth.

Write to me every week. You will do it?

"Yes of course. And maybe I can give you some news soon.

"That is not the one that the war has broken out.

"No, I don't think that's exactly it.

The train whistled for a long time and Helmuth got into his apartment. They were still able to shake hands, looking into each other's eyes, and then the convoy moved away, slowly at first, faster later. Helmuth's last vision of Iolande was there, on the platform, her almost white hair, tanned skin, and red lips gleaming in the light of the voltaic arcs. He would never see her again, but he didn't know it then.

He arrived in Darmstadt on August 2 and reported to the 5th Engineer Regiment. On the 3rd he was already wearing a green uniform, with black insignia on the lapels and white braided epaulettes.

Throughout the month of August he was training a platoon of soldiers and noncommissioned officers, specially chosen, in demolition work, construction of boat bridges, pontoons and in locating mines with new equipment that they had just received.

During all that time he had many occasions to look around him, and when on the 20th he witnessed combined maneuvers involving tanks, infantry, aviation and artillery, he had no doubt that Germany would go to war. Such an expense could only be justified if all that material, all those thousands of perfectly trained soldiers, disciplined like machines, were to be used warlike.

That same night he wrote a letter to Iolande telling her to return to Germany. Knowing that the censors looked closely at all the letters that the Germans sent abroad, and mainly to England and France, he told her that he needed her and that they would marry as soon as he arrived.

On the 24th he received a reply. The insurance company had asked her for ten days to find him a replacement and she was under an obligation to accommodate them. It would embark on the 4th or 5th of September. I was already processing the passage.

Helmuth swallowed. First Lieutenant Remer, who shared his bedroom, looked at him.

"Something wrong?

"He can't come for another ten or twelve days.

"Ten or twelve days does not matter much" replied the other, smoking a cigarette, lying on the bed.

Helmuth narrowed his eyes.

"You think so? You also heard the Führer's speech yesterday.

"He has not said that war will be declared in ten days.

First Lieutenant Remer was a great engineer, but he never stopped to think. He obeyed orders and, despite not belonging to the regular army, did not comment, like other reservists, the orders and the political situation.

They went out into the street after eating. The barracks was located near the railway station. Helmuth stopped at one of the slopes, from which the station sheds could be seen, at the turnoff for the Frankfurt line.

"Look" he said simply.

A huge convoy, of about thirty cars, had just entered the turnoff. The wagons were covered with very tight tarpaulins, but an expert glance could not miss what they contained. They were small caliber guns.

"So, day after day" he said. All those trains are heading to the French border.

"Those pigs won't catch us off guard, well," Remer replied, lighting a cigarette.

"It's not about that". The point is that the power of a country like ours would not be mobilized in this way if there were not a reason that fully justified it.

"I think so" replied the other, peacefully.

Helmuth was looking at the carriages. Soldiers dressed in green, with red artillery emblems on their lapels, wandered between the tracks and stormed the canteen. Their gloved officers, their peaked caps high up at the front and flattened on the sides, their impeccable warriors, all of this made them look martial and tremendously effective.

They continued walking towards the outskirts, towards the field. Fighter jets swiftly crossed the sky, flying in combat formation. Both engineers looked up. Again that wave of pride was invading Helmuth again. It was too much force to resist impassively. Power rises to the head, like wine. No matter how antiwar you may be, when you hear the drum, you set the pace.

Remer's voice snapped him out of his reveries.

"It is useless that we continue to worry. Neither England nor France will give in to the logical German wishes. Poland, that stupid nation, a hotbed of discord throughout its history, will not yield either. We will then have to take it. The Führer has said it and he must know well what he is saying.

"What screams.

"As you like.

They continued their walk. Their arm ached from returning the greetings or offering them. The streets of Darmstadt seemed to have lost all their countrymen or replaced them with the military.

In the evening, both of them off duty, they were in a nightclub on Goethestrasse. It would seem that the war fury had reached there.

The entertainers, the cartoons, sang songs alluding to France, England and Poland, with jokes that became increasingly red as the night progressed. The usual girls hung on the arms of the officers, admiring their new epaulettes, their heavy boots with their trousers tucked into them.

Remer invited two of the girls, who rushed to sit at his table. They ordered champagne, but Helmuth barely licked his glass.

"What's wrong with this one? "Asked one of them while the orchestra harnessed waltz after waltz and march after march, because American music had been banned." Has someone died?

"No one. It is his worried character "replied Remer, who was beginning to be drunk.

He poured a glass of champagne down the girl's neckline and she screamed. Helmuth, disgusted, got to his feet.

"You go? Remer asked.

"Yes. I am sorry. I don't feel like having fun. Do it yourselves.

The hair of one of the busconas had soon reminded him of Iolande's, and it made his chest throb. He was drowning in that atmosphere of screams, smoke and fictitious joy.

He went out into the street. On the way to the barracks he ran into groups of soldiers walking with their heads down. Looking at their faces, the faces of honest peasants, he thought that something was wrong. Not everyone should want war in Germany.

The next morning they were summoned by means of a circular order from the colonel. The entire regiment lined up in a square in the immense courtyard, with the officers in the middle.

The colonel, Von Luvowitz, stood in the middle, saber at his side, head raised.

"Officers of the 5th Engineer Regiment, 32nd Reichwehr Division! Soldiers! I have to inform you that, abusing the good faith of our Recruitment authorities, an undesirable has lived together for a month with all of you, with all of us ... This offense will not go without its just punishment.

"What happen? Helmuth asked a second lieutenant at his side.

"But didn't you find out last night?

"I was out.

"Lieutenant Kronberg. It has been discovered that he is Jewish.

Helmuth shuddered. Kronberg. I knew little about him. She had spoken to him several times and only in passing. He was an excellent engineer, as everyone said. And now it turned out that he was a Jew.

A man had taken several steps forward, within the cadre of officers. Adjutant Hauptmann von Rezske stepped toward him, drums pounding gloomily. Rezske, with two sharp blows, removed the epaulettes and then slapped him, while the other remained at attention. The colonel's voice continued to sound, a high-pitched screech, but Helmuth barely heard what he was saying. He only had eyes for Kronberg's livid, startled face.

The colonel stopped speaking. Two soldiers positioned themselves on either side of the former lieutenant and, following the haunting rhythm of the drum, emerged from the formation. A moment later they broke ranks.

Helmuth returned to his room and collapsed on the bed, still groggy, feeling nauseous. Remer had followed him.

"Well, one less Jew" he said philosophically. The Gestapo will take care of him now. Thunder, you can't trust anyone! I've had a drink with that guy. And now it turns out it was a Jewish pig.

Helmuth did not reply.

As of August 31, he had not yet received word from Iolande. In the early morning of September 1, the loudspeakers of the different units of the barracks began to howl. They all raised their heads startled. The announcer announced that the German Führer was going to speak to his people.

And then, with the voice of the man with the trimmed mustache and the lock of hair on his forehead, they heard the news. The German army, ignoring its ultimatum, had just crossed the Polish border.

The letter reached Helmuth Frick in the railroad car, where he was traveling to the Polish border at Jena, two days later. The letter was dated August 31 and in it Iolande told her that she could not leave England, because the exit visa procedures had been abolished. And he also announced to her, in lines wet with tears, that little Helmuth or little Hermine would be born, if something did not happen to prevent it, in April of the following year.

Remer approached his partner. In his own slightly rude way, he had a good heart and had grown fond of his friend.

"What are you doing, crying? This is not the time, mate. They are waiting for us in Poland, but if that makes you happy... you can lean on my epaulettes to cry more comfortably. Boy, boy, can I do something for you?

Surrounding them was a vast plain whose fields had been mowed for two months. The railway line stretched out before them, like a polished ribbon, gleaming in the rays of the sun. They were in a small village, whose Slavic name Helmuth could not pronounce. This railroad led directly to Lodz and then to Warsaw.

The air was already cool, although the sun was shining overhead. They had been destined to rebuild the road, blown up by the Poles in their retreat.

German troops advanced at a rate of thirty kilometers a day. In front of them, the Polish troops would fall back, fighting furiously, but with utter helplessness in the face of German power.

In a continuous way, the trains loaded with troops arrived at the station. A brief stop to refresh themselves and they continued their march towards the East, like an irrepressible flood.

"I give these guys ten days to surrender," Remer said, as he led the section that dealt with unloading the new rails that would replace the ones the Poles blew up. Is there anyone who wants to place a bet on it?

Helmuth did not answer him. The rails, loaded onto the wagons, had set out. He climbed on top of them and Remer followed suit.

The track had to be fixed in a section of almost two hundred meters. The sapper crews were laying the new cement sleepers and bolting the rails to them. The works were progressing at great speed.

In the distance artillery sounded. German tanks had breached a Polish division in a frontal attack, and then two infantry pincers surrounded the remnants of the division. Thousands of prisoners had been taken and now they walked, encased in their tattered khaki uniforms, towards the rear.

An Adler, carrying the engineer battalion commander, came staggering through the fields to the construction site.

"Lieutenant Remer!

"At your order, sir commander.

"The works are going very slowly. There is an artillery train about to reach that town. It has to happen in three hours.

"Four hours, sir commander," Remer replied tersely.

The commander examined the soldiers who were laying the staves and those who were filling the pieces that were already screwed in with pebbles.

"Okay, four hours, but not a minute more. That artillery has to pass. It is missing up front.

Remer barked a few orders and the soldiers activated the jobs. They worked like automatons, with tired faces, sunken eyes.

"How is the front going, sir commander? Remer asked.

"Well. Have you seen the latest aircraft formation?

"Yes sir.

"It has completely destroyed the entire back of the divisions that were opposing us in Pabjanice. Lodz is on fire and, as I have been told by the Regimental Command, on the roads beyond Lodz you only see retreating Polish troops. Colossal! The tanks advance at full speed, meeting little resistance.

He got out of the Adler and walked over to Helmuth. He was leading a group of sappers who were filling in with earth and cement the place where a high-powered mine had exploded and had produced a large hole in the ground.

"Frick!

"At your order, sir commander.

"Frick, I have personally spoken with Colonel Hübner. I have named you in the part of the day. His work of destruction in Zvice has been a great task. With the death of Lieutenant Colonel Clausen, you are the best wrecker we have in the Regiment, and I have stated this.

"Thank you, sir commander.

The major's eyes were fixed on him.

"What's wrong with him? He is sick?

"No, sir commander. I am perfectly fine.

"Tired, like everyone else, I guess. Well, I would not be surprised if before many hours a gold nail could be placed in their epaulettes. I have proposed it for promotion.

"Thank you very much, commander.

The commander turned and walked toward Remer.

"Is something wrong with Second Lieutenant Frick? He asked in a low voice. I don't want him to get sick now. I need all my men, and more if they are of your worth.

"What happens to you, commander, cannot be fixed at the moment. His fiancee stayed in England without being able to leave there. He hasn't taken the hit yet.

"Already. Have you heard from her?

"He had them four days ago, when we arrived at the border.

"Well, it's not a long time and I don't think the English are going to eat it. The fact that they have declared war on us does not mean that they are going to behave like savages.

"According to the radio, yes, Mr. Commander.

"Radio has been made for the fools and for the short-tempered, Remer. We can tell the German people that the English are scoundrels, but that doesn't mean we buy it. Let Second Lieutenant Frick know that way.

"You must know, sir. You have lived in England for several years.

"Yeah.

"What happens is simply that he loved his fiancée, not that he thinks something is going to happen to her.

The commander decided to stay to speed up the works. The four hours he asked Remer turned into four and a half, but finally, and preceded by a locomotive without drag, to check the resistance of the newly built section, the artillery train passed.

Remer and Frick stared at him. Massive 12-inch guns, mounted on platforms, slowly passed before his sight. Behind each of them traveled the entire crew, sitting on their benches, smoking cigarettes or staring straight ahead.

The sky began to cloud at dusk. A gust of sunset-cooled wind ruffled Frick. Remer handed him a cigarette.

"The commander seemed a bit concerned about you," he told her.

"There is no reason.

"Boy, you don't need to be so dry. I am not one of those English friends of yours who have not let your girl leave the country.

Frick turned his eyes deep in their sockets to him.

"Shut up, Remer.

"I will do it.

The last platform had just passed in front of them. Behind came a train of troops. Through the air, a formation of Messerschmidt flew low, like a flock of goshawks.

The regiment had moved almost to the front line. So close to him were they that a Polish battery, camouflaged in a forest attacked by German grenadiers, fired on them quickly but with little effectiveness.

They had occupied a country house, without giving the peasants time to leave. Helmuth saw them when they were being taken away. The father was a man in his fifties, with fixed eyes, like a bird's. The mother, thick, covered her hair with a yellow scarf, and, finally, a flock of blond children, very frightened, clinging to the mother's skirts.

"The war," Helmuth murmured, looking at the smallest of the children, a baby of about five months, pressed against the mother's abundant bosom.

Their epaulettes were no longer naked. In each of them a golden nail gleamed. Now he and Remer were equal in rank, both First Lieutenants.

"You have just discovered the death of Napoleon. Come on, we can't stay here. They await us in Lodz. This is a city now, not a bloody abandoned village. There will be everything there, even girls.

He was silent for a moment, cut off by the gesture of his companion.

"Nobody demands that you look at them, but I suppose you will allow poor soldiers like us to take a look at them. The ones I have seen so far were not enough to remove the ugliest German peasant girl in the whole country.

Helmuth did not reply. At that moment a Polish grenade exploded very close to where they were. The soldiers fell to the ground, their faces pale. They had only been in the war for seven days, and that doesn't make anyone a veteran.

At last, two German tanks advanced like monstrous caterpillars over the tortured terrain and positioned themselves before the forest. An airplane was flying overhead, pursued by the tracers of a machine gun. This apparently did not prevent him from communicating the position of the battery to the tanks, for a moment later the two steel monsters converged their shots on a particularly thick group of trees.

"Before long they will have removed that obstacle from there" said Remer.

Sure enough, the shots from the tanks silenced the Polish light battery and instantly a section of infantrymen, armed with mausers, hand grenades and machine pistols, rushed into the forest to clear it of soldiers.

Then it was their turn. It was necessary to discover if there were mines, because the forest was crossed by a second-order road, but through which convoys of trucks had to pass.

They found no mines, but Helmuth, walking alongside one of the soldiers carrying the detectors, discovered something else.

That had passed to the infantry. He had the glimpse of a yellowish face, wide-eyed, poking out from among a group of laurels with very green leaves among the orange ones of the other trees.

He also saw something else. Under the face was a rifle, pointed directly at him.

He drew his pistol from his belt holster and fired at the laurels. The soldier walking next to him, detector in hand, threw himself to the ground, believing that he had tripped over a mine.

The face disappeared. Helmuth launched himself into the trees that had concealed the shooter, gun drawn, ready to fire again.

There he was lying on the ground, with his hands on his face. Blood dripped between his fingers and the rifle was lying beside him.

He was very young, almost a child. He was barely sixteen, but he was wearing a uniform. Helmuth called and two soldiers appeared at his side.

Frick leaned over the young Pole and tried to push his hands away from his face, but as he did so his body fell back. Was dead.

Remer appeared, Luger in hand, and stared at the scene. Then he moved his eyes to his partner Frick. It was shaking violently. Remer's rough, rugged face softened.

"I suppose that will be what happens to all of us the day we kill our first enemy.

"Our first murder," Helmuth said through clenched jaws. " Look at that face. Was a kid. A boy, Remer! Child!

They had passed Lodz. This was not a war, but a series of advances only interrupted for a short rest, while new divisions took the place left by those that stopped to rest.

The German tanks found no enemy. Spreading into pincers, attacking head-on, they overwhelmed the Polish army, which until then had been considered well trained and effective. Sure, there was precedent for the Russians in Finland, but in reality, none of the Wehrmacht chiefs had expected the Polish campaign to actually be a military outing.

As it was being.

Helmuth's regiment hardly had time to help build a bridge over a river to replace the one the Poles blew up in retreat, when it had to patch up dynamited roads or prepare sites for heavy artillery pieces to be abandoned in the twelve hours after the front had advanced many kilometers to the east.

Finally, when they were thirty miles from Warsaw, there was a brief arrest. The infantry troops advancing in front of the engineer regiment had come to a halt. From where they were planning a short road to replace one that would take much more trouble to fix, Helmuth and Remer watched couriers on horseback and motorbike speed past them.

The night before, a small rain had fallen, one of the harbingers of autumn that would soon begin. The road was full of puddles that the pale sun had not been able to dry. The wreckage of a Polish fighter plane, which had fallen in combat with the Luftwafe, was visible to his right, turned into a heap of charred scrap metal.

"What will happen? Remer asked.

They approached the commander, who was speaking with the colonel and a group of officers. The colonel pointed forward with a stiff gray-gloved forefinger.

"Some crazy" he was saying. I just heard from division headquarters. They have filled that forest with madmen.

The two lieutenants listened. Helmuth's face was scorched from a mine blast as they were tracked. The ends of her blond hair had been burned.

The captain of a light battery, whose site had just been placed on the ridge, wiped his cigarette from his lips and smiled fiercely. His tunic was unbuttoned, showing his hairy chest.

"Okay" he said. They are crazy. And if this isn't your swan song, I'm willing to eat ten field rations in a row. But I'm not in danger. It will be his swan song.

"What is happening? Remer asked the captain of his company.

"See that forest, Remer?

He pointed to a clear forest of birch, beech, and pine in front of them, at a distance of about a thousand meters.

Between the forest and the knoll where they stood they could see several lines of German soldiers, spread out in a semicircle. Machine guns gleamed in the sun. Small groups of tanks and light batteries could be seen at spaces of about two hundred meters.

Remer nodded.

"Well, the aviation tells us that there are considerable cavalry forces there. If the canyon fell silent, we could hear from here the neighing of as many horses as they have locked in the trees.

"What are you planning to do? Helmuth asked very pale.

"We do not know. What we do know is that the Polish infantry has already retreated, but that cavalry has stayed there.

As if some kind of truce had suddenly been arranged, the cannonade fell silent. And from afar, with extraordinary clarity in the calm air, the sound of a bugle was heard.

Helmuth picked up his field glasses and looked through them. Instantly the forest ceased to be a dark mass in his eyes to resolve itself into a series of trees with branches full of green and red leaves.

Between the logs he made out fleeting flashes of lightning, but they weren't gunshots. It was metal glistening in the rays of the sun.

Another clarinazo, another one, a true concert, diluted by the distance. And then the thunder of the cannon again. The pause was over.

"They already have the machine guns mounted" said the artillery captain looking at the ranks of German soldiers.

"And we," replied the colonel of engineers, whose gray mustache trembled with impatience, "have taken the best location." Gentlemen, we have proscenium boxes.

Helmuth clenched the binoculars with his eyes, struggling to sharpen his vision even more, which was impossible now. Remer took out his own and held them up.

The forest seemed to come to life. It was sudden, as if the trees had suddenly started walking in a performance of Macbeth.

First, a line, green and brown. The uniforms are green and the horses brown. Helmuth watched it advance, smooth at first and rippling later, as the faster horses overtook the others.

And behind, another blue.

"They attack in squads" said the colonel of engineers.

"Better for machine guns" replied the artillery captain, walking slowly towards his cannons, next to which the gunners stood firm, their heads raised, their eyes hidden by the visor of the square helmets.

"Crazy," Remer said sinisterly. Crazy. They are attacking in close ranks.

"Crazy or suicidal," Helmuth replied. Her cufflinks got misty and she took them down to clean them with a dirty handkerchief.

There were no longer two lines that had come out of the forest, but four.

And the fifth was looming.

One of the gunmen, holding a portable radio, raised it to his ear. Then he handed it to the captain.

"Ready" said this. He raised the cigarette to his lips again and leaned over the rangefinder.

"The entire Polish cavalry is there," said the colonel. A bead of sweat had settled on his mustache and he seemed to be falling at any moment. The tension had taken hold of everyone. Helmuth heard a gasp from beside him. It was Remer.

"Get started as soon as possible," he murmured. As soon as possible, damn it, start now. What do you expect?

Now the plain before them had become a dense polychrome mass. Lancers in their strange diamond caps, dragons, hussars, cuirassiers, hunters on horseback... Thousands had come out of the forest and were rushing like an avalanche over the German lines.

The ground shook dullly. Helmuth felt it under his boots.

"A picture from the time of Napoleon," mused the colonel. " Gentlemen, we have gone back in time. Those crazy people are wearing their dress uniforms.

"The swan song" said the artillery captain, finishing maneuvering on the rangefinder.

"A mass suicide," Helmuth replied.

The captain raised his arm and lowered it. The drummer began to speak.

From the right, from the left, others joined the parliament. Helmuth watched as the grenades exploded through the Polish cavalry, opening clearings in it. But the horsemen were closing ranks again and continuing their dizzying march in the direction of the lines of German grenadiers. They were approaching, they were less than a hundred meters from the first line.

"And now" said the colonel "the machine guns. Come on, let's go to them, boys.

It seemed as if he had given the order himself. Smoke billowed from the first and second lines of German soldiers.

Helmuth wouldn't have taken the cufflinks out of his eyes for the world. He looked as if his life depended on it.

The first row of horsemen fell to the ground, men and horses scrambled in confused heaps. Machine guns fired incessantly, exhausting tape after tape, drum after drum.

The second row was mowed down like a gigantic sickle. The third tripped over the fallen bodies and increased the confusion.

"It's horrible, it's horrible ..." Helmuth muttered like a litany. It is awful. That has to stop ...

But it did not stop. No, until the last row of men and horses was on the ground. But the most horrible thing of all is that those piles of human and horse meat were not still. They were not dolls. The most frightening thing is that they were moving, is that you could see horses trying to get up, men fleeing on their knees from the slaughter.

And all in silence, because the roar of the drums firing alongside Helmuth drowned out the brutal neighs, the mind-boggling screams, the moans, the curses. It was a silent movie unfolding before the eyes of the audience.

The artillery captain listened on the radio and raised his hand. The battery died suddenly, but its roar continued to gnaw at Helmuth's ears for a time.

"This is over," said the engineer colonel suddenly. What the hell are those men going to do?

Some fifty soldiers had emerged from the German ranks, hunched under the weight of the apparatus on their backs.

"That" said the artillery captain slowly. They are flamethrowers.

"Not! The colonel yelled. His mouth opened and closed like that of a tragic doll ". That can not be! We are soldiers, not butchers!

A thick silence spread through the group of men. Everyone looked with startled eyes at the maneuvering of the soldiers, there in the distance. An ensign fell to his knees and began to pray aloud:

"Our father who art in Heaven...

A brutal blaze, fifty tongues of fire, erupted from the flamethrowers and went like hooks towards the bodies of the horsemen. A chilling howl, which plunged the air like a knife ...

Helmuth turned his back and vomited. The colonel was shouting something that was not understood, because he was not saying words, but fragments of exclamations, of curses, which did not end.

The flamethrowers cut off their jets, to reopen them. Again the fiery fingers, the hungry tips of the jets of gas, fell on that smoking mass.

"The war" said the artillery captain.

"Not mine," replied the colonel. Not mine! I scream that this is not my war! I scream it!

"For what it's worth" said an engineer major, very pale, as if he too was going to suddenly vomit "I'll tell you that I saw those flamethrowers two hours ago. The soldiers who carried them were SS

"It doesn't work for me! "The colonel howled." Not any of us, professional military men, distinguished specialists! It does not serve us! Because who gave that order that fills the entire German army with crap?

And no one could answer him.

Or did not want.

Warsaw had fallen on September 29. The Russian army, which had begun the occupation of Poland in the East on the 17th, advanced to meet the German. Caught between the two colossi, the country gave in. The news of the surrender reached Lieutenant Helmuth Frick in a Warsaw hospital, where an arm wounded by a piece of shrapnel was being treated in the battle for the Polish capital.

And he also received a letter, which was brought to him by the Swedish Red Cross. Iolande had been interned in a concentration camp for women, somewhere in England.

And then winter. Then the invasion of Denmark and Norway. The battle for the latter, in which the German army overwhelmed the English and French expeditionary forces. When all Norway was pacified, Frick sported two nails in his epaulettes. He was a captain.

And he also knew that at that time, in April 1940, Iolande must have already been a mother, or was about to be one. But it was not until May 1 that he received news from the Red Cross again. In them he was informed that Iolande Zermatt had died a few days ago giving birth to a girl, whose name was Hermine.

With dry eyes, but surrounded by tormented lines, Captain Frick managed to see a Swedish colonel, a representative of the Red Cross. For this he had to overcome some procedures, but the help of the former colonel of his regiment, now a brigadier general, was invaluable. The meeting took place in Berlin, in the Red Cross building. The Swedish colonel received him kindly.

"You already know that we can hardly give any particular information. It is strictly forbidden to us. We can only carry and bring personal news that does not compromise any of the contestants at all.

"But, Colonel, you were in England, weren't you?

Colonel Gustavsson, a man of gigantic stature, with a dry body and worried features, stared at him.

"Yes.

"In this particular case, did you manage to see the woman in question?

Calling the woman in question Iolande, her Iolande, seemed like a ridiculous officiousness, a mockery.

"Yes.

"Why did he die?

"Sorry, I can't tell you. But I can assure you that you have a very beautiful girl. A lovely creature.

Colonel, do you refuse to tell me what were the causes of Fraülein Zermatt's death?

"Not that I refuse, Captain Frick. It is simply that I do not know them. I am sorry. Our mission is ...

"Carry and bring news. And if they are bad, better "Helmuth replied bitterly. Then, seeing the reproach in the Swede's blue eyes, he added.

"Excuse me. You do what you can.

The colonel came out from behind his desk and put his hand on her shoulder. Helmuth was tall, but the other was almost eight inches apart.

"I understand, Captain Frick. Let me tell you one thing: if either side in the dispute had the slightest suspicion that we were biased in our mission, it would be in jeopardy, and many people trust us to take that risk.

"I'm sorry, Colonel. Could I... could I at least know in whose hands the girl is? And couldn't they bring her to Germany?

"I can tell you that you are in good hands, Captain. In very good hands. I have taken care of it myself. I asked to be entrusted to a Swedish family who would gladly take care of her, a family residing in England, but apparently there was an English family who had taken her over. I'm sorry, because that Swedish family might have been able to take her to my country and from there bring her to Germany. Do you have a family?

"No, but me... but Fraülein Zermatt does. I think, at least, it does. I haven't heard from them for a while. Of course I... I would like to keep the girl close to me. That is impossible during the war, but we would fix that.

"Unfortunately, as I told you, an English family had taken her over. However, I promise you, Captain, that I will do my best to get the girl to travel to Sweden. By all means within my reach.

"Thank you, Colonel.

But it was a German captain, who worked in the offices of the German Red Cross, who gave him the news that Gustavsson had not wanted to give him. And then he understood why.

"Fraülein Zermatt died in a hospital in Cornwall," he told Helmuth, having extracted from him the promise that he would not reveal the sources of the information. " A nurse voluntarily neglected her when she suffered from puerperal fever, and even said that if she died, it would be one less boche and that nobody cared about that. I understand that the nurse was Polish. We do not know if it will have been sanctioned or not, but what I do know is that no one with the slightest particle of humanity would do that. And you know, I didn't say anything.

Frick emerged from the Red Cross building at an automatic pace, head lowered, mind empty. So much so that he forgot to greet a lieutenant colonel and he put his foot down and gave him a good fight. He excused himself and headed straight for the barracks. He did not reveal to anyone what he had just learned, but from that moment on he was no longer the same man.

He was doing his duty with zeal, almost fanaticism, and when a few days later German troops entered Belgium, Luxembourg and Holland, Captain Frick was in the front line, taking part in the demolitions of the Belgian forts. When the Germans reached the Atlantic, leaving French forces, Belgians and the entire English expeditionary army in a gigantic bag, Frick wore the braided epaulettes of a commander on his shoulders.

Then, after June 21, the date of the capitulation of the dreaded France, a brief parenthesis began.

"Sit down commander" said the general indicating a chair in front of him. It was a beautiful summer day. Through the window you could see the Seine and the Fiffel Tower on the other side of the river. In the streets there were few people in civilian clothes, and the few who saw each other, passed quickly, looking around them suspiciously. Parisians were still not used to the idea that their beloved city, their Paname, was occupied by Germans and that German laws had to be obeyed, despite the correctness and good treatment of the occupying forces.

"I have called you because I have had very good references from you, Commander Frick" continued the general.

He was a plump man with a clean shaven face and thick eyebrows. Behind his shell glasses, two sharp, penetrating eyes gleamed.

Thank you, my general.

"Your boss, General Curtius, has told me that you are one of the best demolition specialists he has. I will be more precise: the best.

Thank you, my general. I am just doing my duty.

"This is not my news. You go too far in the line of duty. He will tell me that this is the obligation of a soldier in time of war, and I will answer him that people who exceed the fulfillment of their mission are entrusted with positions of greater responsibility, of maximum responsibility, I add.

"Thank you, my general, but...

The other raised his hand in the air.

"We have studied your file, Commander. We have studied it carefully, so there is plenty of useless protests. You will abandon, even temporarily, the Fifth Engineer Regiment, where you have given such high tests of your ability. It is required elsewhere.

Helmuth was silent. I expected.

"I do not doubt that you are comfortable among your former comrades, your former bosses, but the country needs you. You are a soldier and you must obey, even perhaps without understanding the orders.

"Yes, my general.

"You will join a special unit. Your work, Commander Frick, will be absolutely secret. You should not talk about it to anyone, to anyone, understand it well.

"I understand, my general.

"There you will receive the necessary instructions, which are no longer my concern. You will receive the waybill within two days. Those two days are allotted for you to have fun in this Paris that has not yet recovered its appearance, but which, undoubtedly, will offer you plenty of fun.

"If you don't mind, my general, I would like to join my new position as soon as possible. I don't need that break.

"No, no, Frick, these are orders too. Rest, have fun. You were wounded in the arm in the Polish campaign, weren't you?

"Yes, my general, but that is only a memory. IM perfectly.

"Anyway, do it. You already know. In two days, on July 2, you will receive your waybill. Now...

He held out his hand. Frick shook it, stood at attention, and saluted stiffly. Then he left the office.

Paris. He had already been to the city several times, before the war. It was a place he liked, but not now, when its streets were deserted, except for the groups of German soldiers who, camera on their shoulders, traveled from north to south and from east to west. When almost all theaters and entertainment venues were closed or timidly beginning to open their doors.

Two days. What to do during them? He thought of Remer, but Remer, promoted to commander at the same time as he, had his own ideas about what fun is like, and those ideas did not match Helmuth's frame of mind.

Yes, there was something he could do. The Red Cross. That Red Cross that haunted him. He asked for the address in Paris, and that same morning he found himself in front of a towering building with slate roofs on rue Lafayette. He entered and was greeted by a young Swiss-German woman, with brown hair and a pleasant smile.

"There is nothing for you" he said after looking through some files and lists.

Colonel Gustavsson, is he not in Paris?

"No, he is not in Paris at the moment.

"I can not know...?

"Where is? I am very sorry, but we cannot reveal that information.

"Can you at least let him know that I have asked for him? It is he who is aware of my affair.

"Of course. We will let you know as quickly as possible.

He left the signs to which they could notify him, if there was any news, and left the building. He stood at the door, irresolute. He was empty inside and only a kind of impersonal curiosity felt about the new destination, which he would have to join in two days.

He ate in a small restaurant, where there were other German officers, apparently as bored as he, and spent the afternoon wandering through the deserted streets. Every now and then he passed German detachments marching down the road, marking the pace, rattling the pavement with their heavy field boots. He passed the Arc de Triomphe, crossed the Trocadero, walked the boulevards ...

And always with that painful feeling of uninterrupted loneliness. Nothing to think about except Iolande and little Hermine... Was she still alive? Iolande ... dead, killed by the abandonment of a resentful woman from one country who had taken revenge on a poor woman for her resentments against another.

Little by little the indifference turned into hatred. A cold, deadly hatred, like a sword. It was necessary for him to hurt these people. Much damage, as much as possible.

Unfortunately, he was not allowed to take up arms to avenge himself personally, but there were other means. Not only with a pistol, with a bayonet one can hurt those who hurt us. There are other means. A lots of. And he was bound to find one.

The next morning, with the prospect of another day of emptiness before him, and wondering if it would not be better to try to obtain the road map to join again, he received at the barracks, which had been provisionally installed in Passy, the news of that the Red Cross had a message for him. He obtained the necessary authorization to use a car and headed for rue Lafayette. The same Swiss girl attended him.

"I have something for you" he said with his attractive smile. It's a message from Colonel Gustavsson. Personal.

Helmuth put out his hand, which was shaking. The girl gave him a paper. Typed there were several lines.

"Dear Commander Frick, I regret to inform you that all the efforts made to place your daughter in the hands of the Swedish family I told you about have been futile. The family that currently has her has refused to do so, but I can assure you that the child is perfectly well and is cared for as if it were the true daughter of the couple. I renew my feelings for the failure of the negotiations and I remain attentive to you. Sven Gustavsson. "

The creature ... that is, Hermine, his daughter. Frick crumpled the paper between strong fingers. The Swiss girl looked at him with an expression of pity.

Bad news, Commander? "I ask.

"Yes," he answered absently. " For the English.

"How, commander? t

"No, nothing.

Again the English. The family that has it... refuses to give it back. But by what right?

What can they love a little girl for? What are they trying to do with it? Take revenge on me because I'm German?

His eyes glowed with a flame that startled the young woman.

"Can we... can I help you with something, Commander?

"No, thanks.

He came to himself with an effort.

"I am sorry. No, thank you very much, I don't think you can help me. Or ... Maybe yes. I have to leave Paris and perhaps in the place where I am going I will not be able to receive news if there is any. Would you be so kind as to have them sent to General von Berthold at the military headquarters in Paris? He will know how to get them to me.

"Of course I am, Commander.

The girl made a quick note on a pad of paper and looked up at him.

"Are you lonely, Commander? "I ask.

"Very lonely.

There was an expression of sympathy in the brown eyes. If the image of Iolande and that daughter he did not know were not constantly before Helmuth's eyes, he would have asked the young woman if she was also alone and if they could not unite their loneliness the precise time to have dinner and go to a theater. She probably would have said yes. But Helmuth just shook his hand, waved, and walked away. She watched him go with some disappointment. That commander was so young and handsome in his gray-green uniform... He looked so unhappy... With a sigh he turned to face a French woman who had come to ask about her son, a prisoner in Germany.

The tall colonel, who wore a white smock over his uniform, pointed with an outstretched finger.

The sea, the rough sea of the north, shone in the light of a pale sun. But in places where sunlight didn't hurt it, its ripples seemed the color of iron. The waves assaulted the concrete boardwalk.

"We'll find out soon," he said with badly suppressed excitement. It looked like a symbolic figure, its arm outstretched, silhouetted against the gray waves.

Near where the group of men was located there were several barracks, linked together by concrete passageways. The colonel abandoned his gesture and jumped slightly off the jetty.

"Come on," he ordered.

He was striding, followed by the group of officers. Helmuth took one last look out to sea, toward where the jetty ended. A little further from the jetty, there was something that looked like a box. But it was not such, but a concrete platform, with long metal feet sunk into the living rock.

On top of the platform was a kind of quadrilateral, also made of concrete and steel, forming four high walls, with a thickness that Helmuth knew to be fifty centimeters. Fifty centimeters thick of the best cement made in Germany.

A thick cable connected the platform to the mainland. Two of the men in white coats had just spliced that cable to a low-voltage pole.

They entered the first of the barracks. A series of devices occupied three of the sides of it. Before them were tables with more gadgets. Other men, some in uniforms and others in robes, were guarding the devices.

Helmuth walked over to one of the tables and looked into a pressure gauge.

"Ready? Asked the colonel.

"Ready, sir colonel.

The men's gazes had locked onto him. The colonel raised an arm in the air.

"First phase" he ordered.

Helmuth lowered a lever and the gauge shook slightly.

"Second phase" asked the colonel.

"Yes sir.

He lowered another lever and the gauge moved again. This time the little handle was very close to a red streak.

"Now, third phase!

The handle reached up to the red stripe.

The colonel was looking out of one of the windows with binoculars. Suddenly the bunkhouse shook, its foundations seemed to move, and Helmuth grabbed the edge of the table. A deafening explosion shook the lower layers of the atmosphere.

"We did it! "Shouted the colonel." We did it!

A collective hooray! it exploded inside the barrack. Helmuth left his table and went to the window, a simple recess without glass, fitted with a steel grill.

He looked out to sea, over the shoulders of the other men crowding to see.

The concrete platform had disappeared. Around where it was previously, the waves raged down the jetty.

Something stirred furiously in Helmuth's chest. I was there. That was what he had been waiting for so many months. That dreadful, colossal power that had raised an entire steel and concrete construction and had almost volatilized it in midair.

The officers looked into each other's eyes and shook hands feverishly. Their mouths remained open in a stereotypical smile.

The colonel strode toward the door with his brisk, birdlike strides.

Come on, gentlemen. We will see that.

A fine rain began to fall, but neither of them cared. Their gazes were fixed on the end of the jetty. Helmuth, despite the fact that several of those officers were of higher rank than his, caught up with the colonel and ran to his side. He had certain rights to it and everyone recognized it that way.

When they reached the tip of the boardwalk, they stopped. The fine rain prevented perfect vision; but there, before them, no doubt, was a steel bar, emerging from the surface of the sea.

"As if a knife had cut it" said the colonel "As if it had been carved cleanly.

Helmuth was so close to the edge to look that the colonel grabbed his robe.

What do you want, Frick, to take a bath in this icy water? Come on, come on, back off.

The officers had gathered around them. They all looked as if that was the only thing they could do.

"This is work for divers," said the colonel. Gottlieb, get two down and have them sample the material. Have the end of two of the steel joists sawn off and take them to the lab. Can you do it this afternoon?

"I think so, Colonel," replied Gottlieb, Lieutenant Commander of the Navy. Before dark we will have the samples.

"Let's go then. Frick, come with me.

Colonel Stiller had a small office in the second of the barracks. He settled behind his desk and picked up a handful of papers.

"Give me the exact figures, Frick. What tension?

Frick read his notes to him, while the colonel checked them against his. When they finished, he raised his head.

"It's okay. Practically the same. My God, we could have done it a lot sooner if the media didn't haggle us so miserably. But in the face of these tests they will have to bow. They will have no choice.

"I hope so, Colonel.

"Well, Frick, I want to tell you that you have done a wonderful job and that I will let our bosses know.

"I have done my duty, Colonel.

"I know, we've all done it, but you've overdone it. Without your collaboration we would not have seen polygon number one explode today. It was you who indicated the exact quantity of component X-34 and the three alternating phases for the explosion.

He saw Helmuth's gesture.

"Nerd. If you are going to charge the goddess by chance, don't do it. There are no coincidences in modern research. They are over now. Tell the officers that we will celebrate tonight.

His little eyes flashed behind the glasses.

"We have champagne, fortunately. The French wineries have surrendered to us along with their army. See Commander Gottlieb and have your material proof recovery work completed today.

That night all the officers gathered in barrack four, in the dining room. Colonel Stiller presided over the table, his eyes gleaming, his glasses gleaming, and his meager military decorations gleaming.

The waiting soldiers brought the buckets in whose bellies the bottles rested. Stiller took the first.

"Pomméry of 1914, gentlemen. Isn't this a real fluke?

"I doubt it, Colonel, unless your foresight is called chance," Gottlieb replied.

"We are going to toast success" replied the colonel satisfied with the flattery. Sirs.

They rose to their feet, high heels clattering. One captain uncorked the bottles one by one and refilled the glasses, which overflowed with joy. They drank and drank again.

"Gentlemen," Colonel Stiller said, wiping his lips with his napkin. This is a great moment for us, but above all for the German homeland, whose humble servants we are. Our efforts of more than a year have been crowned with success. A partial success, of course, since we have not yet fully achieved our goal, but a stage success that confronts us with the possibility of finishing the work in a short time.

"I hope that now we do not haggle the means to do so" replied a lieutenant colonel with a thick face reddened by drink.

"Gentlemen" said the colonel. I've been on the phone with Hamburg. A tall personality, whose name I will reveal to you in due course, is going to visit this camp very soon.

"Hurray!

"I don't need to tell you what to expect from this visit. At last we have proof in our hands that our efforts were on the right track. The one we call the X-34 component, the most colossal destructive principle ever put into the hands of man, is there, waiting for our bosses to tell us: "Go ahead with him."

"Hurray!

"Commander Gottlieb, do you want to tell the gentlemen in what state the samples of the material taken from the sea after the explosion have been found?

"With pleasure, Colonel. The largest piece of cement my divers found was less than half a cubic meter. The steel joists have been sectioned cleanly at their ends. A subsequent microscopic examination will give us more details, but at first glance the fracture appears smooth and are symptoms of casting. Inside the blocks the steel is twisted.

"And the platform," Colonel Stiller finished, was twenty-five meters long, as many wide and ten meters deep. I leave the calculations to you, gentlemen, to know the destroyed test material.

A Hurray! perfectly timed he drowned out his words. He raised a hand in the air.

"And now, gentlemen, I want us, like me, to toast one of our colleagues, a man who has worked as one of us, but thanks to his industriousness, thanks to his, let's say, genius! These excellent results have been possible. Gentlemen, let's raise our glasses for Commander Frick.

Helmuth remained seated, while the others rose to their feet and raised their glasses, staring at him. His face was expressionless, his pupils fixed before him, in an attitude that seemed modest to Colonel Stiller.

But it was not modesty that Helmuth Frick felt. That was not the prevailing thought. It was of joy, a cold, reasoned joy, the joy of one who after a long time sees his efforts crowned, achieves something that he has ardently desired.

Englishmen, he thought, as the cheers followed one another. "English, your time has come."

It seemed to him that he saw the crowds of office workers with their mushrooms and umbrellas heading to the City, the speakers in the public parks, the peaceful peasants ... All that crowd, which he had known so much and whom he had come to appreciate in another time, had been exchanged for him in so many hideous covers, thirsty for revenge, full of hatred, who had left Iolande to die by placing her in the hands of a resentful woman.

And it was all those masks that had their turn to suffer. Not only was Iolande going to have suffered.

He remembered the summer of last year, when German planes flocked over English towns and cities, the feeling of joy that washed over him when he heard of villages razed by the Luttwaffe, the Stukas swooping down like hawks to the ground. massacring streets, squares and highways, the gigantic bombing planes systematically destroying entire neighborhoods.

Yes, all that, in the summer of 1940, had filled him with joy, but with a joy alleviated by the feeling that this was still little for a people who had allowed Iolande to die. That he had practically murdered her.

And now, he had in his hands the weapon that would make them suffer even more. His pain, his own, had been so buried inside him, without finding a way out, never having tried to confide in anyone, that there were moments when it seemed to drown him.

But it wouldn't drown him.

No, now what was the weapon.

The colonel continued speaking. He was not a military man by profession, but an excellent physicist who had been dressed in a uniform. Therefore, he had no reservations when praising his subordinate.

"Thanks to him we were able to find the exact measurement of the X-34 component, which we still have to call by that name while the secret of its manufacture must remain absolute.

"And that I propose" said the lieutenant colonel "that he be called Stillerita, from now on.

A wave of pleasure washed over the colonel's dry face.

"Not that" he said weakly. I've only been ...

"Its discoverer," replied Helmuth, standing suddenly, glass in hand. " There is no other person, therefore, whose name deserves more to wear the X-34 component. I propose that, if in official documents we are to continue calling this revolutionary explosive by that unknown letter, we should know it among ourselves by the name that Lieutenant Colonel De Beaumont has proposed: Stillerita.

The Hooray! it was thunderous. There were new toasts, but Helmuth only took part in them in a physical way. His mind was far removed from that small town of fishermen in the North Sea, in the Holstein.

Helmuth was able to make a short trip to Hamburg in early October. Colonel Gustavsson had sent him a note saying he would like to speak to him. He asked Stiller's permission, which he grudgingly granted. He needed his assistant and was afraid that the "High Personality" visit might coincide with the leave; but when Helmuth told him that it would only take twelve hours to move to the Hanseatic capital, he gave up.

For the first time in the history of the war the English aviation had bombed the city. It had been a small attack, but its effects were visible on some streets. Entire houses were destroyed, showing their entrails, and the population, surprised, had suffered enough victims.

But none of it mattered to Helmuth, only in an objective way. He had other things to think about.

The colonel was waiting for him in a small building that housed the German Red Cross. He looked even thinner, and deep circles under his eyes narrowed his eyelids. He shook Helmuth's hand and immediately came to the point.

"I have seen your daughter, Commander.

Helmuth's heart nearly stopped beating.

"What ... how is he?

"Perfectly, perfectly, commander. She is a beautiful little girl who must be now... a year and a half?

"Yes sir.

There was a silly question hovering in Helmuth's mind. The Swedish officer seemed to guess it.

"I did not know your mother, Commander, but I do know you. I can assure you that he bears an extraordinary resemblance to you. Do not take it as a compliment, which would be absurd at the present time. It is very much like you.

Thank you, Colonel. It's healthy? Does it breed well?

"I already tell you that perfectly. The family that has her takes great care of her. She has been sent to the field this last summer to avoid him... to avoid the danger of the bombings "he added with a slight hesitation.

"Understand. Has the bombing done much damage there?

"I'm sorry, Commander Frick, but you mustn't ask me that question. We are concerned with the people, not with the results of the war. What you ask of me clashes with our position of absolute neutrality.

"Understand. As for the girl ...

"I have tried to get them to allow their shipment to North America, as they are doing with so many thousands of English children. I must confess that the family that has her has refused to let her go. They seem to be fond of her.

"So fond that they don't want to let you live in a place where there is no danger, is that it? Helmuth asked harshly.

"Don't look at it from that angle, Commander.

"Well, which one should I watch it from? In the United States, which is a neutral country, it would be sheltered from bombs ...

He saw or thought he saw the answer in the colonel's expression. Yes, sheltered from German bombs, he must think. From the bombs of his father's compatriots.

It was cut dry.

"Well, it only remains for me to thank you, Colonel. You have been extraordinarily considerate of me, given that many people need the services of the International Red Cross.

"We do what we can, commander. It is our obligation. There is much suffering, and if we can only alleviate a little ... we consider ourselves happy.

"Thanks again.

"I will keep you updated in the event of a new event, Commander.

"Thanks.

Helmuth shook his hand and left the building. In the transport command he obtained a car, through the special pass that they provided him before obtaining the permit. In it he traveled the scarce hundred kilometers that separated him from his base.

Colonel Stiller was waiting for him in the test lab, a basement built of six-foot-thick concrete walls, interwoven with thick wire mesh. The aeration was produced by powerful fans that expelled the smoke and the air used by holes cleverly drilled in a small cliff so as not to attract the attention of the English planes.

"Ah, Frick, I'm glad he's back now. Did you resolve your issue?

"In part, yes, Colonel.

"I'm glad. Frick, I've been studying your idea. In principle it seems good to me, but we are going to have quite a bit of difficulty to attach the X-34 component, the Stillerita, as you so kindly insisted on baptizing it "added with blushing pleasure", to the small grenades.

Smoking was prohibited in the laboratory. The colonel took out a cigarette, looked at the forbidding sign, and took Frick's arm.

"Let's go outside. If I don't smoke a cigarette I won't be of any use for several hours. Come with me.

They were on the cliff. Workers and soldiers were erecting a new platform at the tip of the jetty. Huge steel tubes were embedded between the rocks at the bottom of the sea, which would later be filled with cement to support the platform.

Colonel Stiller blew a few puffs of smoke into the sea, half covered in mist.

"As our original objective was to use Stillerite as a demolition explosive, none of us had yet thought of using it for small tactical weapons. None of us except you, of course.

"In the memory that I have brought to your attention...

"Yes, yes, I know, Frick. You have presented the approach as you see it. And it seems doable in a way, but there is an abundance of detail, over which you have very briefly passed. It is those details that I am referring to.

He paused.

"And if we are to present that plan to the gentlemen who are to come to see the evidence, we would need an extension.

Helmuth was staring out at the sea.

"Those details, Colonel, will be at the disposal of the lords of Berlin at the moment they request them.

"Then you have them already solved ...

"Almost completely, sir colonel.

"I congratulate.

There was an embarrassing pause and Helmuth turned to his superior.

"At no time, Mr. Colonel, have I thought of exposing my entire plan to anyone without first doing so to you. This trip was the only reason for not having already exposed it to my superior.

Colonel Stiller sighed in relief.

Understand my position, Frick. The head of an investigation must at all times be ready to provide details that the command may request of him. But you will see that I have not bargained at all the merits before witnesses.

"Sir Colonel, I am not ignorant of it, and for that I am grateful to you. We will study it tonight if you don't mind.

"None, none.

He held out his hand, which Helmuth shook. He had won a psychological victory. Without nudging the colonel, his superior had, after all, shown him that the one who was really essential for the job was himself.

And that was very important for their projects.

The "High Personality" were two, actually. A general of staff and another of the SS, who received direct orders from the Führer himself.

When they arrived, in a black Mercedes, with an escort of five other cars and six or seven junior officers, the new platform was ready. It was raining and very cold.

They were greeted by Colonel Stiller, who asked his aides. First, they were shown the designs of the platform and were informed of the progress of the works, as soon as possible, taking into account that neither of them was a specialist.

They examined everything with great coldness, especially the general of the party.

This was the first to speak, apparently claiming to be the head of the mission.

"Don't be surprised by our lack of enthusiasm, Colonel Stiller," he said. For a year we have done nothing more than investigate laboratories like this in which we were assured of having found the weapon capable of crushing our enemies at once.

"Yes, sir," replied the colonel, directing an oblique glance at Helmuth, who stood a little apart, as befitted his graduation, and who only came forward when clarification of some technical detail required it.

"For this reason, before pronouncing ourselves in one direction or another, we need to see the evidence that you, Colonel, announced to us.

The general of staff, while the other spoke, had been observing the designs of the platform and the reports on the materials collected after the first explosion. He looked up.

"Anytime you want, Colonel Stiller.

"Yes, my general.

A concrete tower had been installed, with windows and no glass, but protected by strong steel mesh. Each of the chiefs was provided with a pair of binoculars and climbed the tower.

"Commander Frick is the one who will lead the experiment," Stiller said.

"Let's not waste any more time" observed the SS general "You can start whenever you want.

Helmuth was at his post. He looked at the gadgets that littered his table, altered a pressure gauge or two, more to impress the newly arrived officers than because he actually needed it, and waited for the signal.

"Aren't you a little nervous? Asked Gottliet, the Lieutenant Commander.

"Absolutely. Everything will be fine.

"I confess that I would not like to fail in front of those. The news will go directly to the Führer's headquarters.

"There will be no failure.

A green light came on over the instrument table. Helmuth braced himself. As soon as it turned red, it would be time to start lowering the levers.

Red.

Helmuth seized the first lever and lowered it. Then, with what Gottlieb found infuriating, he did the same with the second. Finally, the third.

Again the ground shook and the gauges shook. The drinking water tank exploded, throwing the water on the ground, and one of the newly arrived officers jumped.

The platform had flown.

The Berlin mission remained at the experimentation base until the partial analyzes of the destroyed materials were known. The general of staff could not contain his satisfaction.

"And this has been achieved with just ...

"Ten kilos of Stillerita," Helmuth replied calmly, anticipating Colonel Stiller. " Ten kilos and two hundred grams, exactly.

"I congratulate you, Colonel," replied the General of Staff, while the SS man held between his fingers a piece of cement, turned into a porous mass that looked more like pumice stone. " This means that with... Gentlemen, we will speak as soon as possible with the chiefs of staff. Such a thing will attract your attention above all other projects.

He turned to Helmuth.

"I congratulate you too, Commander AND... do you think this could be used tactically?

"We are studying it with great interest and speed," he replied.

"Perfectly. We will inform you as soon as possible of what the Führer's headquarters has decided. Could we see the plans to turn this explosive into a tactical weapon?

"Of course. If the general gentlemen serve themselves, follow us ...

In mid-October the order was received at the experiment base for Colonel Stiller and Major Frick to report to the Führer's headquarters in Berlin.

The colonel trembled like a tree leaf.

See the Great Man, even from afar. To be, perhaps, received by him ... "he stammered." Such a great honor ...

"We will see, surely," Helmuth replied coldly.

At that moment he was thinking of those thousands of Polish soldiers killed and doused with burning oil and oxygen. And by an easy association of ideas, he saw the thousands of office workers in the City, in London, with their bowlers and umbrellas, lying in the streets, perhaps volatilized by the X-34 component. His face hardened.

"We must prepare ourselves, Colonel. Who will be in command of the experiment station?

"Lehman, of course. I have to give you instructions ...

"I'll do it, Colonel.

The next day they were in Berlin. They were not received by the Führer, but by Marshal Halder, with his assistants. Halder was already aware of the results of the experiment. They found in him an agile, receptive mind that took care of the problem in general and left the details to his assistants.

"How long do you think it will take to convert that... Stillerita, right? into a tactical weapon, capable of being used on the Russian front and elsewhere?

Behind his words, Helmuth, who was not nervous like Colonel Stiller, saw the fateful word: "rear-guard bombardment."

"The work is progressing with great regularity ... and there are certain obvious drawbacks, on the other hand ..." the colonel sputtered. He turned to Frick as if asking for help. The commander took a step forward, his hands glued to the seams of his heels.

"Six months, Mr. Marshal.

"So much?

"Yes, marshal.

"What is the main drawback?

"The manufacture and placement of the three-stroke escoleta, without the Stillerite exploding. It is a very delicate mechanism.

"Are you the one directing the fabrication work on that fuze?

"No, sir, because manufacturing has not started yet. But I help Mr. Colonel Stiller in the project of its construction.

"Do you belong to the War School?

"No, sir marshal. I belong to the reserve.

"Already.

The marshal briefly conferred with some of the generals around him. Then he turned to Helmuth.

"You will have the works finished in five months.

"Mister Marshal ...

Helmuth seemed to have taken over from Stiller. He seemed incapable of dealing with such lofty characters.

Halder raised his hand in the air.

"No, commander. Germany needs that weapon in five months, not six.

"We will do what we can, sir marshal.

"They will do more than they can. And they will have it finished in that time. I trust in you.

He shook hands with both of them, who bowed deeply. Then he ended the interview.

As they returned to the experimentation base, Stiller looked stunned.

"Five months, Frick... impossible. We can't have it finished in that time.

"It is an order, Colonel. You have already heard the Marshal, Chief of the General Staff.

"But, Frick ...

"We will have it, Colonel. And you can change those epaulettes for a double braid of gold.

"Trust me, that's not what drives me, Frick. It is solely the responsibility ... If something fails in your calculations, in your projects ...

He had an improper start from a military man, but very typical of the scientist that he really was.

"You are the one who should lead the project, Frick, not me!

"With all due respect, I will tell you, Colonel, that this is nonsense. It was you who found component X-34, not me. And that is why it bears his name. We will make it.

And looking at her stubborn profile, her eyes hard and distant at that moment, Stiller realized that, if it was feasible, the man next to him would do it.

They were five months of exhaustive work. Frick checked his calculations over and over again, examined the projects, reworked the job over and over again, until it was exhausted and his collaborators were exhausted.

Meanwhile, the German forces, halted in their victorious offensive by the Russian winter, awaited the arrival of spring to deliver the last, the mortal blow to the Soviets ...

And Japan annihilated the American squad at Pearl Harbor and the United States entered the war ...

And the swing continued in North Africa.

And the Japanese seized Insulindia, dominated English power in Malacca, and waved their flags with the red sun across the Pacific. Finally, in March, on the 5th, after a night when no one slept, the first tactical bomb, of very small caliber, was dropped by a German plane against a moving target in the North Sea. The moving target disappeared, pulverized.

Colonel Stiller could not control the shaking of his hands when the plane returned to the experimental base, and the results were known. The pilot, unaware of what he had transported, was jubilant.

"Colossal" he said. Simply colossal. I was able to place the bomb almost in the center of the moving target, by means of the thrusters. It was as if a hand had suddenly erased the target. I got it right in the center itself, I think. Don't we have a lot of those to go and teach the English how to win a war?

"We will," Helmuth said dryly. And in the meantime, Lieutenant, if you say a single word of this to anyone, not even to your own squadmates, the military police will see to it that you never commit any indiscretion again.

"Yes, sir commander" replied the other very scared.

On the 7th, Helmuth and Stiller moved back to Berlin. Marshal Halder was surveying the Russian front, together with the Führer. As usual, it was unknown when they would return.

"I don't know if I can resist it," Stiller said, wringing his hands nervously. For myself, I would go back to the experimentation base right now to review ...

"There is nothing to check, Colonel, and you know it well," replied Helmuth. Please, Colonel, we must keep calm.

"It is that this force that we have helped to develop... It is so portentous... Until now, concerned with the technical details...

He shot Helmuth a sideways glance. They were both in the dining room of the Terminus Hotel, eating a hideous substitute for coffee and jam that seemed to come directly from the maceration of pine needles.

"... Perhaps we have not assessed the human factor... Perhaps we have forgotten how we are going to use it...

Helmuth watched him silently, his lips pursed.

"Understand well, Frick, that I am not the one at all to criticize our superiors, that idea has not even crossed my mind, but... This force would be so useful in the hands of men to move mountains, drill tunnels, open channels ... What do I know ...

His voice had trailed off under Helmuth's hard gaze.

"That will come later, Colonel. But now, the first thing is ...

He popped the tip of his cigarette against the coffee saucer.

"... Crush England.

"But also to Russia ...

"To Russia, too, Mr. Colonel.

As he did in all his travels, this time he went to the Red Cross building. This time it was not an attractive girl who received him, but a dark secretary, overwhelmed with work.

"Colonel Gustavsson? By God, of course, you won't know. The colonel died, "he said, with some southern accent.

Helmuth's heart began to pound against his ribs.

"He died? He asked a little foolishly.

"Yes, yes, he died. He was traveling in an American plane that was shot down by German airplanes at the beginning of the year.

"I am sorry. Won't you leave... something for me? Major Helmuth Frick. The colonel was interested in a particular matter of mine.

"I can see. Frick?

He reviewed a file and took out a piece of paper.

"Yes, fortunately there is something for you. They look like notes from your own hand. Surely I was hoping to expand on it in some conversation with you. Yes, here is your entire file.

The memo was very short, handwritten, and hastily.

"Let Major Frick know that his daughter is fine. Impossible to get her out of England now that the United States is at war. Maybe Canada ... I can try when I see the W. again. I'm sorry for the commander. He is a good man. Tell her that she is still a beautiful little girl. "

That was all.

So Hermine was still in England, exposed to the bombing. Exposed to hunger, disease... Helmuth clung to the edge of the table, trying to keep her face from showing any emotion.

"Thank you.

The secretary had been looking at the Frick file.

"Of course I do not have Colonel Gustavsson's freedom of movement, but if there is anything I can do for you, Commander ...

"Just try not to lose contact with the ..." W ", it says here. Couldn't you know his full name, by the way? I still don't know who the people who have my daughter are.

The secretary hesitated a bit.

"I don't see the reason why I shouldn't tell you, Commander. Colonel Gustavsson was very scrupulous, but there is really no reason to hide it. Is about...

He looked at one of the documents.

"The John Wilberton marriage and madam. Thirty-eight and thirty-three years, respectively, without children. They live in Southampton. He is a shipbuilding technician. He works in shipyards and lives very close to them.

"Thank you.

"I will take advantage of the first trip to England to try to see your daughter, Commander," said the Portuguese, holding out his hand. Do you want something for her?

"For her? It won't even know that I exist. I don't believe unless they have told you. That could create complications for them with their friends and those Wilbertons. But if I could get a photograph ... Even if it was bad ... any snapshot ...

The Portuguese made a quick note on a pad. Then he smiled.

"If it depends on me, you will receive the photograph, Commander.

"Thank you. In the event that I could return to Berlin, who should I ask about?

By Virgilio Galves. That is my name.

He left the Red Cross. An impressive wind was blowing through the streets of the city, lifting the skirts of the women and the tails of the capes of the soldiers. He slipped into a theater, where he saw the usual burlesque number about the idiotic and regulated life of the United States, the jokes about the English, and many nearly naked women on stage. Disgusted, he left.

Finally, on the 10th, Marshal Halder returned. He received Stiller and Helmuth on the 11th.

"They got it? He asked after firmly squeezing their hands.

"Yes, Mr. Marshal Chief of Staff," Stiller said, shakily. It is done. The tests have been satisfactory, as the Marshal can verify through the reports attached to the request for a hearing.

The marshal, who had not yet removed his saber, picked up the handful of documents and read them quickly. He raised his bright eyes to them.

"In short: a success.

"That is how we can consider it, Mr. Marshal Chief of Staff.

Halder turned to Helmuth questioningly. He knew which of the two was really the important one.

"That's right, Mr. Marshal. One-time proven success. But success.

"Magnificent.

He came around the table and put a hand on Helmuth's shoulder.

"Have they made it public? I mean, who knows, besides you?

"The manufacturing process is known to approximately all our collaborators, Mr. Marshal. The precision system, the fuze and its adjustment, just Colonel Stiller and me.

"You two only?

"Alone, Mr. Marshal. We prefer to keep as secret as possible to avoid any leak, unlikely, but possible.

"Very well done. Could you witness a test in two days?

"Yes, marshal.

"Prepare it. With that test there will be enough.

The test was a complete success. When he finished, Marshal Halder received Frick and Stiller and personally presented them with the epaulettes that they would wear from that moment on. Helmuth's had a gold nail and Stiller's had a gold braid.

"General Stiller, you will continue the work on that experimentation base. Oberstleutnant Frick will leave work here. We need it elsewhere.

It took Helmuth a great deal of effort on himself not to smile. His time had come.

An air general, with a completely bald head and a robust bull's neck, was waiting for Helmuth Frick at the air command in Bremen, Busestrasse, 15.

"Frick? "I ask". I was expecting it this morning.

"I had to go to the experimentation base first, my general. I had to personally take care of the packaging of the pieces to be sent here, following orders from the General Staff.

"Well, the point is that you are already here, fortunately. We have no time to lose, if we want everything to be prepared for the day that was indicated to me.

"May I know what day it will be, my general?

"No, he can't know, Frick. Only I know. Any recklessness could ruin everything. You will find out twenty-four hours before the scheduled time.

"I understand, my general.

"Now let's look at those pieces.

He rang a bell and an aviation colonel entered the office.

"Colonel Ihlefeld, Lieutenant Colonel Frick" said the general. Colonel Ihlefeld is the director of the precision shop. You will report directly to him, Frick.

Helmuth saluted and shook Ihlefeld's hand. This was a very young man, a couple of years older than him, if anything, with a boyish face and brown hair.

"Did you bring the fuzes, Frick?

"Yes, Colonel.

"Have them take them to the workshop. I want to take a look at them.

In the spacious hall, where fifty precision lathes were working, the fuzes were unpacked. There were two of them, about eight inches long and harmless looking.

"Are you planning to dismantle them, Colonel? Frick asked.

The colonel looked at him sharply.

"I've heard a lot about you, Frick, and very good indeed. If you assure me that your fit is perfect, I don't need more.

"I affirm so, Colonel, but I would be much more at ease if you personally verify it.

"You don't want responsibilities, huh? Well, I will tell you confidentially that I don't think there is time for it. The general must have received orders to launch this gossip as soon as possible about some objective that this time will not be a target for practice.

"Coming Soon?

"That's right, Frick.

"But then... won't we build more before launch?

"I don't think there is time. But we have you to keep building them, Frick. See all this machinery? Once we've done the launches, you and I will take this workshop by storm and get to building them at full throttle.

"I find a" but ", Mr. Colonel ...'

Call me Klaus. If we are to work together, it is preferable that we do so.

Well, I find a 'but'. Something can happen to me ... and in that case ...

"Do you mean that no one but you is capable of assembling these devices?

Helmuth did not smile.

"That's right, Klaus. Colonel Stiller was doing the explosive, what we call the Stillerite, and I was adjusting the fuzes.

"A bit of a weird way of working.

"We didn't have too many specialists, Klaus. If something happened to me ...

"I hope it doesn't happen. Anyway, we would always have the explosive.

"Yes, but the X-34 component is somewhat intractable. It is not easily tamed.

"Well, we will start as soon as possible.

The next morning the bombs arrived, divided into sections. According to the plans Helmuth had and his instructions, the assembly began, as quickly as possible.

Two days later it was finished. On a support of oak wood, the two artifacts, devoid of their fuzes, were resting very harmlessly, it seemed.

The general arrived on the afternoon of the second day, accompanied by his assistant.

"Everything ready? "I ask.

"Yes, sir," answered Helmuth. The adjustment of the fuzes must be done in flight and very close to the target, to avoid that any mishap could cause them to explode. It is the only defect in this weapon and it has not been possible to solve it, due to lack of time.

"Are you telling me, Frick? "Growled the general." I just received the order.

The three men looked into each other's eyes.

"When? Ihlefeld asked.

"Tomorrow afternoon. The incursion will be nocturnal.

"But ..." Frick frowned.

What was I going to say, Frick? Something wrong?

"In such a short time I can't really train one of the crew to adjust the fuzes. It is impossible. Materially impossible, my general.

"Who told you that you will have to train anyone?

"How?

"Yes, who told you that you will have to train anyone?

"But...

"You will do it yourself, Frick. Nobody else.

"It is the logical solution," declared Klaus Ihlefeld.

"But... I'm not an aviator. I have not flown in my life.

"That is not the least important," the general rejected a bit dryly. " Nobody asks you to man the device, but to go with the crew to make the adjustment of the fuzes in flight, at the time you are instructed, or that you yourself indicate. That's all.

"But...

"No buts, Frick. You have to do it. That's an order. On the other hand, you should not be afraid of the air. Flying is one of the easiest things out there. Even in time of war. Believe me

Helmuth could no longer object. He bowed his head.

"The two bombs, my general?

"Both.

Ihlefeld put a hand on Helmuth's shoulder.

"You see, you have to go back. We need it here to continue building more of those devices. If it were up to me, I would leave you on the ground, but apparently that's not possible. With that it has to come back. Germany needs more fuzes built according to its system.

"Yes, apparently.

He looked up, until he met the general's.

"Where we will go? I mean, what will our goal be?

"I do not know. It will not be known until two hours before taking the flight. Commander Link will command the aircraft, with Lieutenant Mannheim as co-pilot. There will also be two sergeants, one of whom you will choose yourself, Frick, to help you place the fuzes. That will be the entire crew.

"Perfectly. I choose Mechanical Sergeant Klein. He strikes me as a competent man.

"Well, they can start doing the tests.

The general withdrew. Ihlefeld gazed absently at the two bombs, set on their racks.

"Where do you think you should drop them? "I ask.

Helmuth shrugged.

"That is easy to know. An aircraft manned by four men only should not have a long range of flight. It cannot be, therefore, in Russia, in Moscow, as might well be believed.

"Indeed.

Helmuth's eyes were shining.

"England, therefore," he said.

"Most likely. Got straffe England! Isn't that right, Frick?

"Yes!

There was such savagery in his tone that Ihlefeld turned away in surprise.

"Do you hate the English a lot?

"Like no one in this world, Klaus.

"Do you know them?

"Yes.

He did not add more.

It was impossible to go to Berlin to find out if there was any news about little Hermine, but he got permission to give a lecture to the Red Cross. Mr. Virgilio Galves attended personally.

"Nothing new, Commander" he said. I'm sorry, but the trip I had to make to England had to be postponed for no fault of my own. Anyway, I think I'll be able to do it soon. I have not forgotten your case.

"Thank you very much," replied Helmut, discouraged. " I will appreciate it a lot.

"At your disposal, Commander.

Helmuth slept little that night. There were many things he had to do, and when he was finally able to get into bed at four o'clock, he kept turning the project over in his head.

Sergeant Klein, a lively and resourceful man, had largely understood Helmuth's explanations of how he was to help her. However, the last adjustment should be done by himself, once he is very close to the target.

English aviation, during the air battle over London, had proven to be terribly effective. For every device they lost, nearly three Germans had been shot down, according to reports not made public in Germany, but known to Helmuth.

But it was not the danger they might run once they flew over English territory that concerned him. It was that something went wrong at the last moment, that unpredictable factor that escapes the best profiled projects.

He ran over and over in his mind the possible flaws. There weren't, at least as far as he could.

Sleepless, he turned on the light and lit a cigarette. His hands were steady, on that side there was nothing to fear. Each of those bombs could destroy half a London slum. For example, from Paddington to Marble Arch and Hyde Park, from Edgware Road to the Regent's Park. The two together ...

They were finally going to feel it in their flesh. The previous bombings "Helmuth had seen aerial photographs with the damage produced by the German grenades" would be nothing, absolutely nothing, compared to what was coming.

He imagined it. It was so easy, after having seen the effects of "their bombs" on the test platforms ... If that had been achieved with just ten kilos of Stillerita, what could not be done with a hundred kilos? And with five hundred?

He put out his cigarette. He closed his eyes. An hour later, he still hadn't managed to fall asleep.

The next morning the general summoned him. When he entered his boss's office, he saw that his face was stormy. His robust neck appeared red.

"Frick, bad news.

Helmuth turned pale.

"What is it, sir general?"

"Tragic. The experimental base where you were working with General Stiller has been visited by English planes tonight.

"It's not possible!

"It is, Frick, don't talk nonsense. The facilities have been seriously damaged.

But, General Stiller ...

"Dead, Frick.

Helmuth leaned against the table. His legs refused to support him.

"Understands? I have spoken to the General Staff in Berlin. They refuse to postpone tonight's expedition.

"But, in that case... only I remain of those who know the manufacturing process. This is impossible!

"It is not, I repeat.

Helmuth straightened up.

"I cannot go on that expedition, sir general. You must understand it.

The general fiddled with a pencil.

"I understand that it is not fear that makes you speak like that, Frick, but a sense of responsibility. But now tell me: Do you think that the mechanical sergeant you have chosen is absolutely capable, notice I say one hundred percent capable, of carrying out the adjustment of the fuze in mid-flight?

Helmuth was silent.

"Sees it? Doubt! No, Frick, it has to be you. You and no one else. And it has to come back. Germany needs it.

"Yes, sir general.

"So, let's get to work. The time set for takeoff will be four thirty in the morning. The pilot will know the objective by a closed sheet that will be given to him at the time of take off.

He stood up. He was shorter than Helmuth. He put a hand on her shoulder.

"Come back, Frick. That's an order.

"Yes sir.

And Helmuth left the office slowly.

He was uncomfortable in the flight suit, even though two years of wearing a uniform had made him familiar with heavy boots, helmets, and heavy suits.

They fitted a parachute to his chest and another to his back and taught him how to pull first from behind, and if it did not open, from in front.

They then put on a rubber and cork life jacket, with a valve to inflate it in case it fell into the sea.

The general and Ihlefeld were next to him. The first one said:

"In the very unlikely event that you felld andIn English terrain, if your apparatus were to be demolished, here is this for you.

This was a pack of cigarettes, opened. The general, without hesitation, pointed to two of them.

"These two, marked in red, have cyanide to kill instantly. Don't get caught alive.

"Okay," Helmuth replied, thanking the flight suit that the others couldn't see the shudder that went through him. " I will do so.

"We cannot run the risk of being made to speak if they suspect the bombs. If you throw them and they shoot your plane down afterwards, you could be suspicious. It can't be, Frick.

"I have understood, my general.

Next to him were the pilot commander and his assistant. They were two young boys, of great stature and open countenances. They were both smiling. The two sergeants waited a little further behind, respectfully.

The general took an envelope out of his cloak pocket and handed it to Commander Link.

"You will open it exactly half an hour after taking off. Understood?

"Yes, my general.

"You will immediately communicate the instructions to Lieutenant Colonel Frick. Lieutenant Mannheim will be the navigator, if all goes well. He will be in charge of dropping the bombs.

"Yes, my general.

"Any questions to ask?

"Shall we return as soon as we have dropped the bombs, my general?

"Yes, Link. You will turn around at that very moment. And one thing, Commander: Lieutenant Colonel Frick's life is priceless. It is necessary for me to return to Germany. Do you understand me? If any of you have to stay on this trip, it can't be the lieutenant colonel.

The two airmen looked at Frick with respect.

"We have understood" said Link. We will do the impossible so that the lieutenant colonel returns to the homeland.

"Any questions, Frick?

"No, my general.

"Well then, go ahead. Good luck.

He shook everyone's hands and Ihlefeld did the same. The plane was in the middle of the runway, its engines roaring. Behind him, at regular intervals, were five fighters"Focke-Wulf", the fastest devices out of factories. They would be in charge of escorting him and engaging in combat with the English fighters if necessary. Helmuth knew that a diversionary attack had been arranged somewhere in England, other than where they were going, to distract the English and enable them to carry out their mission.

The hour had come. He got on the plane, aided by one of the sergeants. The place he would travel was the space behind the pilots and the place where the bombs went.

These were placed on a movable platform, above a hatch. The platform served to be able to maneuver with them when adjusting the fuzes. The hatch, to let them fall.

The two pilots got on and took their positions. The dashboards lit up and the checks began. One by one they answered the questions they were being asked from the control tower.

Finally everything was ready. The propellers spun rapidly and Helmuth felt the ground move slightly under his feet.

A moment later they were in the air.

There was a thick glass window next to him. He looked, but couldn't see anything. Due to the English bombardments, which were beginning to be frequent, the city was darkened.

"How long will it take us to leave German soil? He asked Commander Link. He shook his head and indicated the radio. Helmuth took it and repeated the question.

"Half an hour" was the reply.

"And to get to England?"

"Three and a half hours. We fly very fast, sir, lieutenant colonel.

So precisely the moment they reached the sea, it would be when they opened the instruction sheet.

He leaned back in his seat. Half an hour was a very short time. What if I tried to sleep?

But he couldn't. The moment when they would drop the bombs kept replaying. Surely he could see their glow when they exploded, no matter how high they flew. Yes, he had to see it.

He looked at his watch. No more than five minutes had passed. How, if it seemed to him that it had been much longer? But when confronted with the clocks on the pilot's dashboards, he saw that he hadn't been wrong. Five minutes only.

He closed his eyes. A huge explosion. And screams, high-pitched screams, wails, curses. Yes, like the ones I heard in that Polish countryside when thousands of cavalrymen were burned alive.

Ten minutes. But when would the moment come?

An entire neighborhood of London. There, behind him, those two steel monsters contained enough Stillerite to blow up an entire neighborhood. He could imagine all of Soho burned to ashes, blazing like a torch. Or Greenwich, where the observatory was. That would be a good target.

He got to his feet and walked over to where the fuzes were, wrapped in a thick layer of foam rubber.

Sergeant Klein approached him respectfully.

"Already, Mr. Lieutenant Colonel?

"Not. Not yet, "he replied dryly.

He sat down again so that the other did not notice his nervousness. He wanted to smoke, but he didn't want to. There was no danger, but discipline had to be observed.

Twenty minutes.

He peered over the shoulder of the pilot commander. He turned and smiled at her.

"How high do we fly? He asked over the indoor radio.

"Four thousand meters, Mr. Lieutenant Colonel.

"Will we have to raisernos more?

"No, I don't think so, Lieutenant Colonel. It is the fixed height and, except for complications "he smiled", we will not do it.

Twenty-five minutes... God, how slowly time ran!

The pilot glanced at the dashboard clock. Then the copilot. He nodded and took the controls. The pilot, with exasperating slowness, took the sealed sheet from the pocket of his flight jacket and looked at it for a moment before opening it. Helmuth restrained himself from yelling at him to hurry up.

At last, it was open. He read it and turned to Helmuth.

"Southampton, Sir Lieutenant Colonel. The Southampton Shipyards.

Helmuth came to himself painfully to the pilot's questions. He was questioning him if he had been dizzy and if he was okay.

"Good ... I feel very good" he replied.

It had been like a daze, as if someone had hit him on the head. Only now was he painfully recovering from the blow.

"But ... that can't be" he said.

"It is written very clearly, Mr. Lieutenant Colonel. The Southampton Shipyards. Or as close as possible, of course. That means that the English will try to intercept us, of course, and that we may have to fight. Then...

But Helmuth couldn't hear him. Link's voice sounded like a beating of drums to him, but those drums were in his brain.

No, no, that couldn't be. Hermine was there, in Southampton, in the city he was tasked with destroying. No, it couldn't be. Fate plays these games on a man. Man could not defend himself against a fate that did things like that.

"Mr. Lieutenant Colonel ...

Link and the copilot looked at him strangely. The two sergeants had approached as well.

"Are you feeling well, Lieutenant Colonel? He needs something?

And the fact is that they were already in the sea, they must have already been flying over the waves. And Southampton would be there, three hours away in time. It is not many three hours for the man who has the mission to murder, to tear his own daughter to pieces.

The pilot commander had risen and was crouching toward him.

I had to hide, no I had no choice but to hide.

"I'm fine, Link" he said. Go back to your post, please.

"But if I can do something for you, Lieutenant Colonel...

"Everyone go back to your posts. It's already over. It was a momentary dizziness.

Link obeyed, his face troubled.

He could give the order to return, of course. But what would the general say? A girl cannot stand in the way of German victory. Not one, but a million, would be sacrificed if necessary to achieve victory for eighty million Germans.

But Hermine was not the general's daughter. It was his, his!

He felt the daze again. He had seen what happened to steel and concrete when the Stillerite exploded. What would happen to those delicate meats ...?

I couldn't think about it! Return? Impossible. There was only one solution left, only one. He couldn't drop those bombs. I could, yes, drop them, without adjusting the fuzes perfectly. He knew the way to do it. They would not explode, but then the English might find out the secret, and that was not what they wanted.

No, the bombs had to fall into the sea. Sea. At the bottom of the Atlantic Ocean the secret would die. And then he could go back to making other ...

But no, I couldn't go back. That was impossible. They would judge him as a traitor (traitor him!) No, he couldn't go back.

Then he was the lucid man again, the orderly, methodical brain. He was faced with a problem and Helmuth Frick, faced with a problem, became a thinking machine.

He took the handle that electrically opened the hatch in which the bombs rested.

"Watch out, Mr. Lieutenant Colonel! Sergeant Klein said uneasily. That is the command of ...

His mouth widened, like a surprised fish.

Helmuth Frick had lowered the grip.

The plane jumped, freed from a thousand kilos of step, and Link fought for a few moments to take control of the controls again. He had been taken completely by surprise.

"But, what happened...!

The hatch had automatically closed again. Helmuth stepped to the exit door and removed the pistol from its holster.

"I have dropped those bombs into the sea" he said calmly, facing everyone. I didn't want them to explode over Southampton.

Link passed the controls to his copilot and got to his feet. A stupefaction impossible to describe was reflected in his features.

"But... Mr. Lieutenant Colonel...

"That is what I have done. Link, go back to Germany. And tell them ... Lieutenant, put down the radio or I'll shoot you!

Mannheim, the co-pilot, released the radio switch as if it burned him.

Tell them my daughter is in Southampton. If you want proof, ask Virgilio Galves at the Berlin Red Cross. Then they will know that I am telling the truth.

"But you don't realize what you've done! They will form a military council to all of us! They will shoot us!

"No, if they do what I tell them. Not from One more step, Link, or I'll be forced to shoot you, and I don't want to! Stay where you are.

One of the sergeants was putting his hand on his hip. Helmuth pointed the pistol at him as he felt behind him to find the handle that opened the hatch.

"One more move and I kill him.

Then he found the crank, turned it, and leapt into the void.

It was a moment of infinite anguish, until he dropped the pistol and frantically tugged on the parachute strap. A tug that nearly broke her shoulders and she found herself floating in icy darkness.

He also opened the second parachute, to slow the fall, and inflated the life preserver.

He didn't know how long it continued to fall, slowly. The roar of aircraft engines faded into the distance.

And, finally, the water, the water even colder than the air. The lifeguard held him afloat well.

"Your last hour" he thought. You won't get out of here alive.

The minesweeper HMS Leslie found him two days later, in a state of almost complete exhaustion, but still alive. The Leslie's captain gave him the first care, one of which was trying to thaw him. When he could speak he asked who he was, and Helmuth told him.

"Lieutenant Colonel Helmuth Frick, of the German Army," he replied. " The plane we were in was destroyed over the sea.

"I didn't know," replied the Leslie's commander, a kind of red-bearded pirate. " Anyway, there have been several of your planes that we have shot down. Well, you will explain all that to my superiors.

"May I ask what port you are taking me to, Captain? Helmuth asked calmly.

Southampton. What more does one port give a prisoner than another?

Well, believe it or not, Captain, I do care. In Southampton I have a daughter.

He turned to the wall and fell asleep instantly.

END